AN ALIEN FOR CHRISTMAS

Empaths of Lyria

REGINE ABEL

CONTENTS

AN ALIEN FOR CHRISTMAS

The best gifts come in big packages.

Meet Kathleen: a thirty-six-year-old Plain Jane extraordinaire, with a Ph. D in Xenobiology and another in Spinsterhood. This year, yet again, her sorry self is stuck working on Mars for the holidays. Aside from dodging the unrequited attention of a certain cringe-worthy bachelor on the station, she mentally prepares for yet another lonely and boring Christmas.

But when her sister sends her an early gift in the form of a drool-worthy alien hellbent on fulfilling her every desire, Kathleen isn't so sure she wishes to stay off the naughty list anymore.

DEDICATION

To all the introverts who get tired of trying to justify why they are actually happy just chilling at home or being by themselves. To all those who understand that there is such a thing as overstaying one's welcome.

To anyone who ever got shamed for how they look, how they dress, or what they like to eat. True happiness doesn't come from the approval of others, but from learning how to love oneself.

You will never find true beauty until you acknowledge the one staring right back at you in the mirror.

CHAPTER 1
KATHLEEN

Of all the times 'the Dick' could have picked to loiter in the hallway, it had to be now. I barely managed to step back into the connecting corridor I'd come from and plastered myself against the wall to avoid getting noticed. I needed to go to the lab to feed my little experiments, but Mr. Blabbermouth had to block the only way out of the residential sector.

Wilson Dickens—AKA 'The Dick'—was the bane of every single female's existence on the base. He believed himself some sort of cock in the henhouse when it came to non-mated ladies. You'd think with my plain looks, challenged sense of fashion, and nerdy disposition, he'd be turned off and keep walking. Buuut nope! The Dick was relentless and somehow had a homing beacon where I was concerned.

Right this instant, he had Patty cornered and was drowning her in an ocean of verbal diarrhea. Mind you, she was quite the gossip fiend as well. However, even in the split second I'd spotted them before taking cover, I'd recognized the glazed over stare that meant she'd had enough. You had a better chance of getting a mosquito to not bite you by scolding it than you had of getting Wilson to shush. He was probably bragging about the circumference of his biceps, or the impressive weight he could bench press. We had all heard it at least a million times and gave even less of a shit today than we did the first time he brought it up.

Chewing my bottom lip, I cast a glance back at the corridor I was standing in. If I backtracked, I could use the maintenance tunnels to get to the industrial sector of the base. Like everything else here, the tunnels were clean and well-maintained.

Blyde—named after the corporation that had built it—was both a mining and research base on Mars. While the limited activities quickly became fairly repetitive, the state-of-the-art base was the perfect playground for the super geeky. We had minimal supervision, and lots of leeway as long as we produced results.

As one of the top Xenobiologists here, I needed to get my shit together and not lose my privileges. My sorry butt was stranded here for the holidays because my current experiment was deemed very important to the corporation, and results were far from stellar lately. First, I needed to go feed said experiment before it keeled over. But I wouldn't get that done by standing here like a dummy in the hallway.

Annoyed by Wilson's voice still droning on in the main corridor, I decided to retrace my steps and head towards the maintenance shaft. But just as I was going to push away from the wall I was still leaning against, the door at the end of the corridor parted open revealing the base's supervisor, Philip Stelthen. I barely repressed a groan. This was all but a conspiracy against me.

"Kat?" he called out with a slight frown. "What are you doing there? Are you okay?"

Son of a... Could he be any louder?

Mind racing, I tried to come up with a reasonable explanation as to why I was randomly leaning against the wall at the end of the corridor. Obviously, I couldn't say that I was hiding like a wuss from the unrequited attentions of The Dick.

Taking a few steps towards him, I gave him a reassuring smile while rubbing my nape. "I'm fine, thank you," I said, loudly enough that he would hear me but hopefully not so much that the others would as well. "I just had a bit of a dizzy spell, but it's all gone now."

"Dizzy?" he asked, with concern. "Are you sure you're fine? Should you go by the Infirmary?"

I groaned inwardly again. Philip had only two volumes: loud and very loud.

"No, I assure you, I'm totally fine."

Even as I spoke those words, my heart sank upon hearing Patty bursting out laughing from the connecting corridor. If only I hadn't delayed in hauling ass out of here as soon as I had noticed Wilson's presence, I'd be long gone by now.

"Is that Patty?" Philip asked. Without waiting for my answer, he immediately moved ahead to the intersection to waive down the two people I'd been trying to avoid.

"Hey Phil!" Wilson called out.

"Hey Will," Philip distractedly replied before turning towards Patty. "Hey, Patty, we need your first responder skills. Kathleen is unwell."

"Oh gosh, Philip. I don't need first aid. I just got dizzy," I whispered forcefully, utterly mortified.

He totally ignored me while waving the others to approach. I moved forward, meeting them halfway to show them that I was totally fine.

"What's wrong, Kat?" Patty asked with the same look of concern Philip had given me earlier.

"Nothing's wrong. I just had a brief dizzy spell, and Philip blew it all way out of proportion. I'm okay."

"You're not pregnant, are you?" Patty asked, while touching my cheeks and my forehead with the back of her hand.

"What? No! I'm not pregnant," I exclaimed, staring at her disbelievingly while the two men gaped at me, Wilson with an air of betrayal, and Philip as if I had grown a second head.

"There's nothing wrong with being pregnant," Patty said reassuringly.

I batted her hands away from my face.

"I. AM. NOT. PREGNANT," I repeated, glaring at her. "I just happened to have skipped a meal. My blood sugar got a little low. I have to go feed the Kirdies, and then I'll grab something to eat," I continued in a reasonable tone.

"Oh, okay," Patty said, looking a little disappointed.

The wretched gossiper was only bummed out because she'd lost a juicy topic that would have fueled the rumor mill for a while. Wilson's relief, like a man who'd just found out his girl-friend hadn't cheated on him after all, made me want to punch him in the throat. By itself, his overly prominent Adam's apple naturally made me want to smack it in.

"Well then, we must feed you at once," Philip said in a tone that brooked no argument.

"I was just on my way to the cafeteria," Wilson said with a bit too much enthusiasm. "We can have dinner together!"

"That's an excellent idea!" Philip said.

Fuck that!

"I can't," I replied politely. "I have to go feed my experiments. I didn't give up on spending the holidays with my family only to let the Kirdies kick the bucket," I said, fighting the urge to tell them all to just piss off, I didn't need a mother. "Now, if you'll excuse me, I'll go take care of it right away, and then I'll grab some grub."

"No, I will take care of feeding your critters," Philip interjected. "I've done it before for Josie when you were on vacation, and she needed the evening off. The feeding charts are up to date and still at the same location?"

"Well... yes, but—"

"No buts, Kathleen," Philip said in a stern voice. "You neglect yourself too much, and it is my duty to make sure my staff is doing well. If you continue on this path, I will have Patty check in on you daily to avoid you damaging your health."

"Gladly," Patty said with a serious, motherly look.

As the base's Personnel Coordinator, her role was a mix of human resources, event planner, and supply manager. Although it appeared like a lot, she actually twiddled her thumbs often as everything was pretty much automated and events cycled through a handful of different types that didn't require all that much preparation.

"No worries," Wilson said, making no effort to hide his triumphant smile. "I will take very good care of our little Kathleen. This way, my dear."

He gestured towards the hallway, puffing out his chest. I'd never wanted to slap anyone so badly. For a split second, I considered arguing that I would just take food back to my quarters, but I'd only get another earful about needing to socialize more. With two-thirds of the base home for the holidays, management insisted that the few people remaining mingle to avoid depression.

Clenching my teeth, I gave Wilson a stiff smile, while secretly cussing out all three of them. The four of us walked together down the hallway to the industrial sector of the base where the cafeteria was also located. I brooded in silence while they all happily conversed about the presents they were either hoping for or planning on sending their relatives on Earth or elsewhere.

We split up as soon as we passed the currently vacant guard station separating the industrial sector from the residential one. Normally, the guards made sure no visitors entered that private area unless they were accompanied by an actual resident of the base. Since only residents remained as part of our skeleton crew for the next few weeks, there was no point manning those stations.

With the others gone, the hard soles of Wilson's shoes resonated loudly on the polished concrete floor. It wasn't surprising. Everything about that man sought to draw people's attention. If he could have ridden a motorcycle inside the base, he would have had the eardrum bursting, super loud mufflers to make sure everyone noticed him passing by. His clothes, a bright orange, skin-tight t-shirt on top of a second skin of a black leather pair of pants, also made him standout.

To be fair, The Dick wasn't hard on the eyes ; quite the opposite. Tall, and broad-shouldered, he'd been the cause of many exploded ovaries on Blyde. Like most of the women here, I'd felt weak in the knees the first time I'd seen him. The man was buff, with muscles for days, a drool-worthy bubble butt that demanded to be squeezed, a dreamy, manly face that could have earned him a main role in Hollywood, and the kind of rumbling voice that wetted panties and made toes curl. But the minute he opened his mouth, that was it: game over.

"You really need to take better care of yourself," Wilson said in a chastising tone. "You are far too important to us to fall ill because of poor nutrition. I'm going to make it my duty to look after you from now on."

"Oh, that's *really not* necessary, but thank you," I said, horrified that he would seize this as an opportunity to further harass me with his attention. "I don't normally skip meals, and I was going to take care of it anyway, had Philip not intervened."

"Well, I'm glad he did. A pretty girl like you needs someone to pamper her," Wilson said indulgently.

It took every ounce of my willpower not to roll my eyes. Not only was I not pretty, but I also definitely didn't need to get pampered. Well… okay. I could use the pampering but not by him.

"When I need to get pampered, I go to the spa," I dead-panned as we approached the large set of doors of the cafeteria.

They parted before us, revealing a massive room with enough tables to sit three hundred patrons. It was one of three cafeterias on the base, the other two being far smaller. Since a lot of people took their food to go—preferring to eat at home or at their desks—we never faced a seating problem. Even when everyone was back from vacation, the staff's flexible schedule ensured enough people ate at different hours to avoid unmanageable crowds.

Like everything in the base, white, light greys, and chrome dominated for the color of the walls and the furniture. For hygiene purposes, it was easier to detect problematic areas that way—not that we had any complaints on that front. The cleaning bots did wonders. The base was so clean, you could literally eat on the floor.

The rectangular room possessed three distinct sections. The biggest one surrounded the buffet, the medium catered to meals a la carte, and the final one had special tables surrounding a hot plate where patrons could either cook their own proteins or have an android chef prepare their entire meal in real time. Wilson started heading towards the latter, but I made a beeline for the buffet, forcing him to follow suit. This wasn't a date. Eating at those hot plate tables meant we'd be here for hours. I just wanted to chow down on something already prepared and get the heck out of here.

Wilson pursed his lips in disappointment. I almost felt guilty... almost. Being in the mood for some comfort food, I filled my plate with a large portion of lasagna, a roll of garlic bread with melted cheese, and a small chef salad. I eyed the desserts, and the strawberry shortcake winked at me something fierce. However, I decided to be semi-good and wait until I was done with the main course. If I could still breathe after that, I'd come back and grab something sweet.

Normally, I would drag my feet and pick a little bit of everything. But this time, I made haste to finish my selection first and choose our table. I picked a free one near other occupied tables. Wilson would have selected an isolated one to broadcast the false narrative that we were on a date. He regularly used these types of tactics to get his prey to feel almost obligated to play along.

I settled down and politely waited for him to arrive before touching my plate. In the meantime, I poured us each a glass of water from the bottles already sitting on the table. When he finally took his seat in the chair next to me around the round table, I couldn't help but stare at his plate. It was always a wonder to me how such a bulky guy could achieve this type of mass judging by all the rabbit food he ate. It was funny to have the traditional case of the woman eating salad while the dude enjoyed the steak be reversed with Wilson.

However, just as I was peering at his food with amusement, he was eyeing mine with disapproval. That obviously failed to gain him any additional brownie points—not that he had any to begin with.

"That's a lot of carbs," he said matter-of-factly, although I didn't miss the chastising undertone.

"That's a good portion of lasagna," I deadpanned. "But you sure enjoy a lot of grass," I added mockingly before shoving some of the tasty pasta into my mouth.

"It's not grass," Wilson said haughtily. "It's steamed vegetables, roasted potatoes, and a grilled chicken filet. Just the right diet to give my body what it needs to remain lean and build muscle mass. As you can see, it is yielding very nice results, if I may say so myself," he added, spreading his arms and looking at his own body.

I didn't roll my eyes, but my face spoke volumes. "Tell me, Wilson," I asked while cutting another piece of my lasagna. "When is the last time that you have genuinely enjoyed a meal? I mean, are you seriously salivating looking at your plate? Are you telling yourself 'Oh, my taste buds are going to have an orgasm with this meal!' or are you simply thinking 'This is one of my rations for the day?'"

"Food isn't where I get my orgasms," Wilson said with a suggestive face that made me nauseous.

"You know what I mean," I said, giving him a stern glance. "James is also a fitness freak. His body is to die for, but he doesn't eat like a rabbit."

"You're not James," he retorted with a shrug. "You clearly don't have his metabolism, and truth be told, his isn't all that great either. I could teach him a thing or two. And if you placed yourself in my care, I could help you achieve as hot a body as mine."

"Wow, way to force a woman to have dinner with you just so that you can food and body shame her. You sure have a way with words. Please, do go on. You're making my toes curl," I said sarcastically, not in the least offended or hurt. I didn't care enough about his opinion—in fact, not at all—and I already knew how diplomatically challenged he was.

"I'm not body-shaming you, love," Wilson said as if speaking to a difficult child. "You know I care a great deal about you. I just want to help you achieve your fullest potential. You very much know how hot I already think you are. But you could be so much hotter still, and then we'd be the sexiest couple on Blyde!"

I just gaped at him for a moment, unable to believe what I was hearing. First off, I wasn't hot by any stretch of the imagination. Aside from my Plain Jane face, the fashion gene had never found its way into my DNA, and my tummy and my ass were a testament to my love of potatoes and pasta. I wasn't ugly, merely so plain I faded into the background. Instead of becoming a Xenobiologist, I should have become a pickpocket; no one would have ever even noticed I was there, having my thieving little way with their goods.

"Okay, first off, I never was and never will be a fitness freak," I said in a stern voice. "Second, I happen to be quite comfortable with my very normal body. Sure, I could lose 30 lbs. and be at my ideal weight, but I've grown quite fond of Mr. Pudge," I said, leaning back in my chair to squeeze the fat around my belly with both hands. "So, anyone who intends to date me will have to love Mr. Pudge, too, because we come as a package."

"You named your belly fat?!" Wilson exclaimed, his blue eyes bulging and his plump lips parting in shock. It made his square jaw appear even broader. But even then, the bastard remained handsome. Such beauty was wasted on that asshole.

"Dude, you have no idea how many parts of my body have been named," I said before taking a bite out of my garlic bread, the melted mozzarella cheese stretching just the way I liked.

I chewed with an almost malicious glee as Wilson gazed at me, his wheels turning as he no doubt attempted to guess which body parts—aside from the obvious ones—had been baptized.

Thing was, for all his apparent rudeness, I'd come to realize Wilson's bluntness was just a manifestation of his social ineptitude. It confused the heck out of me, too, since *I* was the introvert and the nerd, yet still managed to interact normally with people when needed. Wilson, obviously a jock, should have mastered the social thing but was epically failing instead.

"Third thing," I said, after swallowing that mouthful, "you and I are not, have never been, and never will be a couple. That *one* date I consented to with you confirmed that we are totally not a match. So, I would really appreciate it if you would let it go."

"But—"

"I'm not done!" I interrupted, knowing that once he started talking, it would be a never-ending flow. "You're into fitness, sports, healthy living, fancy clothes, gambling, and clubs. I'm a nerdy homebody who loves movies, reading, board games, video games, and especially her baggy clothes. You have high ambitions while I'm happy with my current career."

"You only feel that way because you've never had anyone to show you a good time," Wilson said with a dismissive wave of his hand. "Training is challenging for people when they don't have a partner to motivate them. Fashion is another way to feel good about yourself and show others how fabulous you are. I can teach you all of that, and then you'll get hooked. Again, if you let me take care of you instead of hiding in your hole playing those silly games, this could be the start of the new and improved you."

This response just left me speechless. The idiot was so self-absorbed, rather than trying to sell me on how he could meet me halfway, he was more focused on dismissing my preferences to convince me to become like him.

I shook my head and just stuffed my face with the absolutely delicious pasta. Even as he droned on about what a wonderful life we could have together, I tuned him out to enjoy my meal. I finished the last bite with great sorrow. However, Mr. Pudge couldn't handle the desserts that had been calling out to me, whispering all the naughty things they'd do to my taste buds. Oh well, next time maybe.

"So," Wilson said with the eagerness of the salesman hoping to close the deal, "what do you say about us giving it another go? I mean, we can take it slow if you're not ready for a commitment. Seeing how we're both single, we can still have a good time while getting to know each other better."

I gaped at him in disbelief, surprised I didn't spit out the sip of water I had just drunk. My mind was feverishly working on the perfect way of telling him that I'd rather use a cheese grater shaped like a dildo to scratch any itch I may have than to let his wiener anywhere near my hoo-ha. Just as I was opening my mouth to give him a scathing response, my personal com rang. A brief look at it showed it was my sister calling.

"Sorry," I said, actually relieved not to get into an unpleasant argument with him. "It's my sister calling from Titan. I must take this. Thanks for dinner… I think. I'll see you some other time."

Without giving him the chance to respond, I almost ran out of the cafeteria.

CHAPTER 2
KATHLEEN

I answered my sister's call only long enough to tell her that I was on my way to my place, and to call me back in five minutes. With her fancy job, she had unlimited long-distance calls paid for by her employer, whereas our number of minutes were limited. Clarisse was my older sister. I was the second child, and we had a little brother, named Richard who still lived on Earth with our parents. Although we were a close-knit family, Clarisse and I had always been two peas in a pod. It was quite strange, too, considering how opposite we were, with her being the super extrovert to my extreme introvert.

As soon as I got home, I nearly stepped on my wretched little Worf. No bigger than a kitten, my little Fudian had a completely different type of cuteness. He looked like a little green troll, with very short legs, long thick arms, an impressive little beer gut, and massive black eyes devoid of sclera that took up the entire sides of his face, leaving no room for cheeks. He had no nose aside from two tiny little dots for the nostrils, a slit of a mouth decep-tively inconspicuous. When he opened it, he could literally split his face in half and extrude crazy sharp teeth that would even cut through metal. Otherwise, he kept them resorbed and just gummed the heck out of everything. Like he did just now, as soon as I removed my shoes.

Worf had an obsession with chewing on my big left toe, which I ended up naming Chewie. He would just latch on and refuse to let go, even as I walked around the room. Since it cracked me up, I usually let him have his way. Half dragging him, I stepped into my living room located left of the entrance and turned on the giant screen on the wall. It immediately announced an incoming call, which I accepted.

The beloved face of my sister appeared, grinning at me from ear to ear. I loved the brat, although I usually called her a high maintenance diva. As always, she looked gorgeous with her dark brown eyes delicately highlighted by a perfectly applied black eyeliner, and a burgundy lipstick that nicely contrasted with her cinnamon skin without screaming for attention. While we both inherited the reddish-brown color of our mother's hair, we had gotten my father's kinky hair. Clarisse always did wonders with hers; I was just content to let them do whatever they wanted.

"Hey Clare!" I said warmly. "Girl, I so owe you one right now."

"Hey Sis! Really? What did I do?" she asked.

"You just saved me from Wilson."

"The Dick?"

I burst out laughing. "The man himself! He was totally trying to drown me in a sea of verbal diarrhea."

"Oh wow. Is that the stench I'm smelling?" Clarissa asked, teasingly.

"Could be! Then again, it could be your cat's litter. Your pet's intestines always seem to be in an advanced state of putrefaction," I teased.

My sister made a face at me but didn't argue. Her pet seriously had the foulest farts on this side of the galaxy. But her

Maine Coon was a serious beauty—and a major white fur shedder.

Getting back to Wilson, I gave her a quick summary of what had just happened. She couldn't help but roll her eyes and shake her head.

"I can't believe that douche tried to body-shame you!" Clarisse said, anger descending on her features. It made me all warm and fuzzy. My sister always turned into quite the mama bear when people messed with her younger siblings. "And I especially can't believe you told him you'd named your tummy Mr. Pudge. We *really* need to talk."

I smirked, unrepentant. Lifting the hem of my oversized shirt, I pinched the sides of my navel, releasing and squeezing them again to make it look like a talking mouth.

"Listen here, Missy," I said, taking on a deeper, masculine voice. "This is Mr. Pudge. Kitty-Kat and I are BFFs. No matter what she does or where she goes, I will *always* be there. So, anyone who wants to be with her will need to be with me, too, cuz I ain't going nowhere!"

Clarisse shook her head again, looking discouraged. "You're hopeless."

"Guilty as charged," I said, releasing Mr. Pudge and letting my shirt fall back down.

"That said, you're far too nice, Kitty-Kat," Clarisse said in a disapproving tone. "You need to put that idiot in his place. I'd have mopped the floor with his ass a long time ago."

I chuckled, enjoying that visual in my mind. For all her polished appearance, my sister didn't mess around with idiots. "I know. I know. But I hate confrontations. And frankly, he's harmless, just annoying as fuck, like a certain someone I know," I said, glaring at Worf.

The adorable pest was having a field day chewing on my toe with his gums. I lifted my leg and shook it to try and make him fall. Worf immediately latched on, holding onto my foot with both his arms and tiny legs. He emitted a grumpy growl to tell me to behave. I chuckled and shook my foot again. My sister facepalmed on screen, which only made me laugh even more. It was one of many recurring games between Worf and me.

"Seriously, woman, you need a far less disturbed pet than that little menace," Clarisse said disapprovingly.

"Leave him alone. He's adorable!" I said, protective of my little brat. "But you can send me one of those fancy alien chew toys from Titan for him so that he can give Chewie a break," I added, letting myself drop on my comfy three-cushion couch.

Wrapping my hand around Worf's bulging gut, I yanked him off my toe and placed him on my lap. He glared at me, but his growl turned to a purr the minute I started rubbing the bone ridges on his forehead. They were the reason I'd named him Worf, as they reminded me of those on the forehead of that character in an old classic sci-fi Earth series.

"Speaking of which, I've already shipped your Christmas present," I said.

"Oooh!" Clarisse said, clapping with excitement. "A whole lot of Martian treats?"

"Yep, as promised. *And* a whole lot of new ones you've never tasted before," I added with a grin.

"Whoop, whoop," Clarisse said, pumping her hands in the air. How she managed to still look elegant and classy doing that remained a mystery to me. But she quickly sobered. "On a sadder note, I'm guessing that means you're not coming over for the holidays?"

"Nah," I said with a sad face, while rubbing Worf's tummy. "I'm having a hard time with my latest experiment. Lily, the Kirdie mother, is rejecting Mirik, one of her newborns. The worst part is that Mirik is the only one who actually displays the evolution traits we'd been trying to splice into that species. I've been feeding him manually, but I fear he will die without her caring for him. So, anyways, my ass is stuck here."

"That sucks. I'm really sorry to hear that. But I know you," Clarisse said encouragingly. "You *always* find a solution. You'll make it work."

I smiled at her, my heart filling with love for my sister. As weird as she found me, Clarisse was always there for me, supporting me in whatever endeavor I embarked on.

"Thanks, sis," I said affectionately.

"Too bad, though. Remember Alan, the guy I'd been seeing for the past few weeks?" Clarisse asked, her face taking on an unusually sheepish expression that had all my juicy-gossip-incoming alarm bells going off. "Well, it got unexpectedly serious fast, and we've decided to move in together."

"NO WAY?! That's awesome!" I exclaimed, genuinely happy for my sister.

Truth be told, I didn't understand how she wasn't already married with two-and-a-half kids in tow. Granted, she was picky —with good reason—but Titan only welcomed the elite of the elite in every possible field.

"Thanks," she said with the most adorable shy grin. "He was really looking forward to meeting you. And I was quite eager to introduce you to a few very nice bachelors."

"Oh God, spare me!" I replied with a horrified look. "Every single blind date I went on was a complete disaster. Plus, who in their right mind would want to move from the fancy, largest moon of Saturn to the dusty surface of Mars?"

"You could move here," Clarisse suggested in a hint-hint kind of way. "You're super smart. I could get you a job in no time."

"No thanks!" I said in a tone that brooked no argument. "You guys are too posh for me. I bet you not a single store on Titan sells oversized, comfy shirts."

Clarisse snorted. "Right you are. But I still think you need a man that's not The Dick. Anyway, what do you want for Christmas?"

"Send me the perfect man, gorgeous with a hot body, a big cock, who loves to chill at home, watch movies, play video games, and doesn't mind getting his toes chewed or his stomach booped by Worf."

"Booped?" Clarisse asked, with a confused expression.

I chuckled and waved my hand dismissively. "I'll explain another time. Failing to find Mr. Perfect, you can send me the kinkiest, most twisted collection of sex toys from Titan to convince Wilson his services are not needed."

"Really?" Clarisse asked, slightly taken aback. "We do have some adult stores—"

"No, silly! I'm just kidding!" I said, laughing. "If I ever did something so stupid as to show The Dick a sex toy collection, he'd assume it was a disguised invitation for him to use them on me."

My sister scrunched her face as if she'd just smelled something foul, making me laugh again.

"Bad visual. Really bad visual," Clarisse said with disgust.

"Agreed! But, kidding aside, you know my tastes are simple: comfy clothes, those crazy action movies and series from Titan and Alpha Centauri, and chew toys for my brat," I said in a more serious tone.

"Okay, got it," Clarissa said. "Comfy clothes, movies, toys for the weird pet, snacks, *and* a secret surprise coming your way!"

"Oh boy, surprises from you usually spell trouble," I said, feeling both worried and excitedly curious. "At least give me a hint!"

"Nope! Got to go. Love ya!" Clarisse said in a singsong voice.

"Love ya," I replied with a grin before the screen went dark.

~

When Saturday came rolling in a couple of days later, I decided to get a bit of work done from home. I had a truckload of reports to write. Milan, the base's junior lab assistant, was on duty over the weekends to look after the live creatures in the various labs so that we could relax. If anything went wrong, he would poke me.

The Kirdies were a species commonly found on multiple planets of the Alpha Centauri solar system. They'd been imported to Mars for their ability to detect rare minerals and dig tunnels to them with infallible precision. My job was to enhance them so that they would fare better with Mars' atmosphere. Using those creatures significantly reduced the prospecting costs of the mining conglomerate I worked for. Baby Mirik was the first successfully born enhanced Kirdie. Finding a way to keep him alive and thriving was my top priority. Failing would put me in a less than pleasant position with my employer.

By the time my stomach started clamoring for food, the thought of cooking felt beyond unappealing. Going to the cafeteria required getting dressed and putting on at least a partially human face, which was even less appealing. Therefore, I settled on ordering in. The options were limited, but it beat making something myself or going to fetch it.

For a split second, I considered changing clothes. As was my wont, I was wearing sweatpants and a far too big t-shirt... no bra. I stared at my chest while chewing on my bottom lip, debating whether to go put one on. Did it even make sense to put myself through that torture since I'd be taking it off after the delivery guy left? My boobs were perky enough that they could fool the dude into thinking I actually had a bra on. My nipples were also behaving, not poking their heads out and drawing unwanted attention to them. I could totally get away with this. Plus, it wasn't a beauty pageant. Chances were Jules or Nia would be delivering, and they'd seen me more than enough times in my 'I-can't-be-bothered' outfits.

With that decision made, I went right back to work. Sitting on the table next to my laptop, Worf was staring at the screen with an intense gaze as if he was evaluating my report—which he, of course, couldn't.

I barely repressed a happy squeal when my doorbell rang a little less than fifteen minutes after placing my order. Worf tapped his belly like one played on percussion instruments, and his sharp teeth extruded from his gums at the prospect of some munchies. The wretch knew he wasn't supposed to eat human food but always managed to steal a piece—or ten—from my plate.

I hurried to the door, ready to receive my food. But the door opened on Wilson's obnoxious face, holding two meal boxes.

"What the fuck?!" were the only words to come out of my mouth.

"Tsk, tsk, Kathleen," Wilson said in a disapproving tone. "That is no way to greet your guest bringing you food."

"What are you doing here?" I asked. "Is that my order?"

"I was on my way to ask you out for dinner when I ran into Jules," Wilson said with a smug smile. "I told him I was on my way here. So, I took your order, bought one of the dishes on his hovercart for some other client, and came here."

"You took someone else's meal?" I exclaimed.

Wilson shrugged. "It's just a chicken salad. Jules already has another one getting prepped for that client. They won't even notice the delay."

I inwardly cursed at Jules and made a mental note to tell him not to pull that shit again in the future. "Well, that was very kind of you to bring me my meal, but I do not have time for company right now. I'm in the middle of tons of reports. So, I'm afraid you will need to find yourself someone else."

"I'm sure those reports can wait until you've had time to relax a bit while enjoying your meal," Wilson said dismissively. "After all, you still owe me the other half of our dinner date since it was so abruptly interrupted by your sister's call."

This time, I didn't refrain from rolling my eyes. "First off, it wasn't a *date*, and I don't owe you jack shit. Second, I've tried really hard to be nice about this, but I'm starting to think you're a masochist. Why else do you keep forcing me to turn you down? This is really beyond unpleasant. I am *not* interested in dating you, or banging you, or doing whatever else with you. Please, stop hounding me!"

"Why are you being so obtuse?" Wilson asked, looking at me like I was some strange alien. "I have no mental issues, but I'm starting to believe you might. All this isolation isn't normal. This systematic refusal to get physically or romantically involved with a healthy, apex male is abnormal. I'm trying to help you. Were you the victim of some sort of trauma that—?"

"Oh my God! That's enough, Mr. Wannabe-Shrink," I said, interrupting him. I yanked my meal box from his hand. "Thanks for bringing my food, now go away. And don't come back to my quarters again."

I tapped the wall interface, closing the door in his face, and walked towards the table to put down my food. The doorbell rang again. Fuming, I emitted a growl of annoyance that had Worf immediately go into protective mode.

I marched back to the door, Worf hopping down the table to follow me. "I said go away!" I snapped at Wilson as soon as the door opened.

"I'm not done talking to you," Wilson said, outraged.

"I don't care. *I* am done talking to *you*. Now, get! If you ring that bell again or knock, I'm unleashing Worf on your ass," I threatened.

I never lost my cool like this. I couldn't say if my conversation with Clarisse or having finally reached my breaking point had triggered my anger, but I'd had it with his harassment.

He snorted with disdain. "That crippled Fudian is your protector? Damn, woman, you're even more far gone than I thought. What's with the aggression? Are you in your grumpy week?"

I stared at him in disbelief at such cruel words. Yeah, Worf was crippled. He'd been born with stunted legs, which kept him from working as a herd protector like his species normally did on various alien farmlands. I'd adopted him so that he wouldn't be euthanized, and never regretted it. But my little brat had more than overcome his shortcomings, and one would be a fool to underestimate how badass he was.

And right now, my little Fudian was pissed.

"You are truly a poor excuse of a human being," I ground through my teeth. "I'm in the I'm-about-to-punch-you-in-the-throat week. So, get the fuck out of here before I file a formal harassment complaint."

"Excuse me?" he exclaimed, taking a step forward.

Big mistake.

Worf emitted a single, vicious bark and inflated nearly ten times his size. His mouth opened, displaying the double rows of terrifyingly sharp teeth. Wilson yelped, taking a few steps backwards. In his haste, he stumbled and fell to the floor, spilling his salad over himself.

"Next time, I'll have him bite your balls off. Now clean up that mess and leave," I snapped before closing the door in his face.

I looked down at Worf who deflated back to his normal size. He stared at me with a smug expression on his little face, his bulging belly pushed forward in his version of puffing out his chest. I picked him up and kissed his bony head before bumping his belly with my forehead.

"Boop!" Worf said.

"Boop!" I responded affectionately. "Thanks for protecting me, my little hero. For that, you get to steal some of my food."

He didn't understand complete sentences, but he got the general idea that I was proud of him, and that food would come his way.

He grinned.

CHAPTER 3
ANDERS

My eyelids fluttered, and my lungs filled with air for the first time in many months. It confused me that I would be pulled out of stasis before my current learning cycle was completed. According to the visual display on the interface of my chamber, I had a couple of language modules not started yet, and my current one still had 12% remaining.

The door of my stasis chamber slid open with a discreet hiss. I flexed my muscles as life slowly returned to them. Jarak—one of the rare Lyrian Patriarchs—hovered over me, checking my vitals. Simultaneously, he extended a cup for me, no doubt containing a stimulant to get me back up and going in seconds. I sat up and turned to the side of the cushioned surface I had been lying on, my legs dangling as I gratefully accepted the beverage.

"Why did you wake me so early?" I asked in a grumpy tone, my voice a little rougher than usual from months of disuse. "You missed my irresistible charm this much?"

Jarak snorted, his usually overly serious features softening with an amused smirk. "Hardly. You are too much trouble. I'm only waking you in the hopes of getting rid of you," he added mockingly.

My eyes widened at that comment. Of all my brothers, I had been deemed among the least likely to find a partner because of my 'idiotic' sense of humor and my systematic need to not follow protocol. I couldn't argue with that assessment, but I didn't consider that a flaw. What fun was there in being predictable and conformist? Still, his words implied the algorithm had finally found a match for me. That the Seeker had expressed interest in my profile made me giddy with excitement.

"I have been matched?" I asked, making no effort to hide my enthusiasm.

"Drink first, we'll talk after," Jarak said.

The way he said that, and the fact that he immediately busied himself with whatever was displayed on his datapad had all of my alarms go off. I downed the sweet and minty, clear blue liquid. It tasted as fresh as it smelled, soothing my parched throat as it went down, and whipping me into a full state of alertness.

My gaze roamed over the Stasis Hall A, one of five—at last count—each containing five hundred of my brothers. From my vantage point, the walls of the octagonal room resembled a honeycomb with each alveola showing the bottom of my brothers' chambers. It displayed their name, vital signs, date of stasis initiation, whatever learning programs were currently in their queues, and their progress in their active one. A few chambers were being taken out by hovering lifts. My heart warmed for them at the thought that they, too, had been paired. With luck, they would approve of those pairings.

My eyes shifted towards the Patriarch who had turned back to face me. Like all of us Lyrians, he was tall and thin, with facial features mostly undefined. His glowing, white eyes stood out against his skin that resembled liquid silver. The size and placement of his horns, the shape of his crown—the bone ridges adorning his forehead—and the length, thickness, and shape of his two-pronged tail were some of the main distinguishing features of our species. But the true identity signature was his aura. As Empaths, the Lyrians' perception of others relied mostly on their aura and emotions.

And right now, the Patriarch's emotions clearly expressed that something was a little wonky with my pairing. Me being me meant that instead of freaking me out, it intrigued me all the more.

"Come, Anders," Jarak said, before heading out of the room.

I followed in his wake, curious to hear about my potential mate, and above all to feel her aura to assess our compatibility. To my surprise, when we exited the Stasis Hall into the main hub of the Hive, instead of taking the right corridor towards the Visitors Hall, he led me straight ahead to the Screening Office. Observing the protocol for Fledglings, I walked a few steps behind him.

I opened my mouth to question that direction but immediately felt him hardening as he prepared to decline answering anything before he was ready to do so. Scrunching my face, I kept silent. That reaction from me surprised him as much as it did me. I normally utterly failed at not speaking whatever thought crossed my mind, regardless of my counterpart's emotional state. That was not exactly a positive trait in an Empath whose entire existence was meant to please a mate.

We entered the large room at the end of the hallway where a single Patriarch was supervising the work of a handful of my Fledgling brothers—although none of them were my actual siblings. Each one was sitting at an individual station with a couple of monitors to replay videos recorded by their Seeker and to study their psychological profile. Beside their desk, a 3D holographic projector allowed them to visualize the physical appearance they would choose based on their Seeker's preferences should they proceed with the pairing.

That, too, made me giddy. From the moment of my birth, I'd wondered which species I would become based on my chosen mate. Alpha Centauri had such a wide variety of species from blob-like to quadrupeds, aquatic to flying, cave dwellers to nomads, and everything else in between. I had no preference. I just wanted to finally feel that spark that made my heart soar and my soul sing—a partner whom I would want to be empathically bound to for the rest of my life.

Instead of taking me to one of the free workstations, Jarak led me to a private one with a closed door. Those were usually reserved for Seekers occupying important political or intergalactic positions and who required discretion during their search for a partner. Had I scored such a high-ranking person? That didn't make sense, not with my troublemaker reputation.

Jarak gestured for me to take a seat in the chair in front of the workstation inside the small room and settled across from me in a guest chair—which was normally never present. He gazed at me with an oddly paternal expression. His conflicting emotions were starting to worry me.

"As you have correctly surmised, we have received a request for which you were deemed the best match," Jarak said carefully. "The fact that we are here instead of the Visitors Hall also allowed you to guess that there is something unusual about this situation."

I cast a curious glance at the left monitor that only displayed 'Kathleen Wright' and a file number. That was an unusual name. I couldn't think of any species in Alpha Centauri with individuals named like that.

Jarak smiled. "Her species is only one of the unique aspects of this potential pairing," the Patriarch said in an unusually kind voice. He was usually pretty direct—not cold or hard, just to the point. "Kathleen is a human from Earth, a planet located in the Solar System, the closest planetary system to ours."

"A human!" I exclaimed, blown away and thrilled at the prospect of being partnered with someone completely different from what I'd grown to consider the norm. That was right up my alley. "I have vaguely heard of that species, but I didn't know we had started mating with them."

"There are extremely few cases—less than a dozen," Jarak conceded. "All of them are with humans who have relocated here, in Alpha Centauri. However, the main reason this case is unusual is that Kathleen did not initiate the request; her older sister Clarisse did. She wants the perfect mate as a Christmas gift for Kathleen."

My jaw dropped, and my brain froze. For the first time in my entire existence, I was speechless. There was no such thing as 'gifting' a Lyrian Empath to someone. We weren't toys, pets, or random merchandise to be purchased. A rigorous selection process ensured the pairing was perfect for both partners as once bonded with their Seeker, the Lyrian Empaths could never mate with or love another. I couldn't decide if I was more offended that the Patriarchs—and likely Matriarchs—would have considered this an option for *me*, or more curious to get to the bottom of this whole thing.

"I sense your hurt, son," Jarak said softly. "Do not be upset or offended. You are one of our sons. Despite your unusual personality, we love you equally and want nothing more than to ensure your happiness."

While still a little uncertain how I felt, the sincerity of his words was undeniable. The affection emanating from him took me by surprise. Not for the first time, I wondered if Jarak was my sire. I would never know and suspected he didn't either. As he was one of the ten mates of my Matriarch, there was a 10% chance he could be. But where my thirty-four siblings each displayed character traits that could be matched with one or more of our Patriarchs, mine differed completely.

"We initially declined Clarisse's request. But her persistence made us curious," Jarak said. "Considering she had already thoroughly filled all the forms and provided some video recordings of her sister, we figured why not toss it in the Screener and see what happens?"

"And the Screener said the weird request is a perfect match for the weird Lyrian," I concluded for him, still on the fence about this situation.

"The Screener stated you were a 98.7% match, which is the highest we've ever had for you, or frankly anyone else," Jarak said in a reasonable tone. "For that alone, we felt compelled to inform you of this request."

"Wow! That is *very* high," I conceded, my curiosity starting to take over my bruised feelings. "But there's more, isn't there?"

The Patriarch nodded. "Yes. But we can discuss that after you've had a first impression of the female. If you do not feel any connection, then the rest is a moot point."

My contrary personality almost made me argue, but my curiosity about Kathleen took precedence. Jarak leaned forward to launch one of the recordings. It first displayed the image of a bipedal female with a coppery skin, puffy, reddish-brown hair, thick eyebrows, light-brown eyes, a perky nose, and generous lips. The loose clothes she was wearing made it difficult to properly assess the anatomy of her body. Still, it looked fairly similar to ours with flat feet, two legs, and two arms with five-digit hands.

"Humans come in a great variety of shapes, sizes, and colors," Jarak explained. "They have two genders, but their pairings aren't always male-female. Every combination of couplings can be found, sometimes including three or more partners. But this specific candidate would want an exclusive male-female pairing."

I nodded, curious to find out more. Her appearance neither excited me nor did it turn me off—which was normal. That had zero bearings on our attraction to an individual. Next, the video displayed a series of stats about her, including age, height, weight, education level, languages spoken, career, current location, pet name and type, etc. It struck me as odd that she would be stated as biracial when both her parents were humans. The nice bit of information though was that humans averaged a lifespan of 120 years. With her being thirty-six, this meant we could have quite a long time together. That pleased me greatly as my lifespan would sync to hers.

The video finally moved on from photos and textual info to actual footage of Kathleen. It was a video call with her sister. Although I hated not being able to feel her emotions, her personality immediately pleased me. She struck me as quirky, irreverent, quick to humor, and non-conformist. Kathleen pretending to make Mr. Pudge speak to Clarisse made me chuckle. Watching her try to shake off Worf made me laugh. In both cases, it earned me weird looks from Jarak. Some additional random footage showed her eating some brown paste called peanut butter with a spoon. In another, she was sitting on the floor, wearing undies but no pants, instead of on the couch her back was leaning against.

"Why is she on the floor?" I asked, confused.

"The floor is heated. Her pet enjoys the heat. She imitated him a couple of times and has apparently developed a taste for getting her bottom warm and toasty," Jarak explained with a 'What can you do?' expression. "She certainly is a weird one, but I assure you most humans are more… standard."

"She's not weird," I said, slightly offended on her behalf, but beyond thrilled at the prospect of meeting her. "I think she's awesome! Standard is so boring and predictable. I definitely want to do an empathic test with her."

"I always knew you were a weird one," Jarak said teasingly before his face took on an apologetic expression. "Unfortunately, empathic tests are not possible. Kathleen isn't even aware of your existence or that you are looking into her. Clarisse's entire goal is for you to be a surprise gift."

Each of his words felt like a bucket of acid being poured over me. I stared at Jarak in outrage and disbelief.

"So, where does that leave me?" I asked in a clipped tone. "You expect me to make a lifetime commitment based on a written bio and a few videos? What if the minute we meet in the flesh, I'm repulsed by her aura?"

"Calm down, Fledgling," Jarak said in a slightly sterner tone. "You should know better than to make such assumptions. Your attraction and sense of compatibility with this female is the *only* factor that should determine the outcome of this potential pairing. No one will push you into blindly bonding with this female, especially with a species we are still fairly unfamiliar with."

I breathed out in relief and nodded. Gratitude filled my heart that despite this odd pairing, my welfare remained the focus of our parents.

"Due to the unusual nature of this situation, I brought it to the attention of the Matriarchs before waking you," Jarak continued in a gentler tone. "They have agreed that should you feel a genuine attraction to the human, we would make an exception for you and allow you to leave Lyria without binding to your final form."

My jaw dropped, and I stared at the Patriarch, convinced I had misheard him. "You would let me go to her unbound?" I repeated to make sure my mind wasn't playing tricks on me.

He nodded slowly.

"Why would you possibly consent to such a thing?" I asked, utterly floored. "What is so special about this female that the Matriarchs would consent to break one of our core rules?"

"There are multiple reasons," Jarak said. "The main reason is that you are already forty years old. Until today, you never got a match exceeding 63%. If you aren't mated by the age of fifty—"

"I will no longer be able to sync my lifespan to that of a potential mate's and will die within the next five years. Yes, I know," I said, more worried at the thought to have never truly lived than I'd ever admit to.

Jarak nodded. "The other reason is that, although there's nothing special about Kathleen, per se, her species is of great interest to us."

That got my attention.

"You must *not* let that second reason influence your decision in any way, shape, or form," Jarak warned. "Bonding with someone who is wrong for you will not only make both your lives miserable, it will also defeat the purpose of us investigating new possibilities."

"Humans?" I asked.

"Yes. They are an untapped market for us, and a massive one at that," Jarak admitted. "Our presence here, in Alpha Centauri, is well established, but not at all in the Solar System. Due to their formerly excessive population on Earth, humans have colonized most of their neighboring planets. Many of those living away from their home world or from Titan are having a harder time finding a life mate. A successful pairing between you and Kathleen could open the door for more interest among humans. Too many of your brothers are currently in stasis waiting for a match. For some of them—like you—the clock is ticking."

I nodded slowly. I'd never considered humans as potential mates as they were such a foreign and distant species. This could indeed be a wondrous opportunity for both humans and Lyrians.

"But once again," Jarak cautioned, "this must *not* influence your decision. The union must be beyond successful to stir the interest of other single humans. If not you, another will pave the way in the Solar System. For now, I will leave you to study the rest of the material provided by Clarisse regarding her sister. Take as much time as required. Temporary quarters have been assigned to you until you've reached a decision whether to proceed or return in stasis."

"Thank you, Patriarch. I would indeed like to study her

profile and the human culture more thoroughly," I replied, excitement resurging within me.

Jarak nodded then walked out of the room, closing the door behind him.

I turned back to my screens and tasked the artificial intelligence of the system to find me all relevant files, videos, and tutorials related to human courtship, relationships, marriage, culture, etiquette, and general social interactions.

While it performed the query, I watched all of the other videos provided by Clarisse. Oddly enough, I found myself replaying over and over that video call with her sister with Worf chewing her toe. Every time, it made me smile. The second video that kept me hooked was labelled 'Kathleen's bad karaoke' where she was singing a series of human songs. I'd personally found her voice quite lovely, but after comparing it with the original performances, it became clear why humans would consider her singing terrible. And yet, I could listen to her for hours.

In light of the tons of files queried by the A.I., I elected to have them compiled into a training sequence that I would process in sub-sleep—the semi state of stasis that still allowed our brains to function and learn, while slowing down our other vital functions to a state almost similar to hibernation.

As it would take a while to process the file, I started playing a little with the 3D avatar modeling system. It allowed me to experiment with the type of physical appearance I would give myself should I decide to go through with this.

You already know you are.

Yeah, I did. Unless something really horrendous came out of those human culture and ritual files, I was pretty set on going. There was something enchanting about Kathleen's quirky personality.

However, I had little to go on about her preferences in men. I believed Kathleen had been mostly serious about the description she'd given Clarisse of the ideal male she wanted; meaning a handsome man with a perfect body, and a big cock. But what was the perfect male body?

The Grecian model seemed to be the most universally accepted. It accounted for a variety of body ratios with the waist being 45-47% of the height, and shoulders being 1.618 times the width of the waist, among others. Except, what was Kathleen's ideal height for a man? Then came the nitty gritty. Humans had a billion different shades of skin, hair, eye color, hair texture and length, shapes of noses, eyes, mouths, cheekbones, ears. Even their fingers, nails, knees, and feet differed. Then there was the matter of body hair. Some men had next to none while others could pass for furry beasts.

Normally, such issues were avoided by the Seeker giving us a clear description of what she—or he—wanted. The Fledgling would simply show her a 3D mockup and the Seeker could request adjustments until the perfect result was obtained. I was shooting blind. Thankfully, as I wouldn't be bound, if she disliked the appearance I settled on, I could change to something more to her taste. This not only removed a huge weight from my shoulders but also made it more fun to experiment with possibilities.

Initially, and for lack of specific guidance, I made a dark-skinned male to match her complexion. My completed model looked pretty good, even observing the facial symmetry, which was considered a requirement for beauty on Earth. I'd also selected some curly black hair, not as tightly curly as the darker humans, but also not as straight as the paler ones. I didn't see it as a cop out or lack of commitment, but as a pleasant mix of both.

However, I suddenly realized that the analyses of her entertainment preferences heavily skewed towards a certain pale-skinned actor. Her records indicated she had watched every single one of his movies and serial shows and re-watched quite a few of them a disturbingly high number of times. Further research deemed him the heartthrob of the ladies, and he had won Most Handsome Man of the Year award three times in a row. Although she had other male actors and performers that seemed to appeal to her, that one seemed to be her favorite. I, therefore, made a new model inspired by him.

Pleased with myself, I saved my work and went to my temporary quarters to learn everything about courting a human.

CHAPTER 4
KATHLEEN

I sighed in despair while bottle feeding Baby Mirik. The little Kirdie was too small and too weak compared to his siblings born of the same litter. His wrinkled pink skin almost looked translucent. In direct contrast, his siblings had thick skins, almost beige, and were already showing the first signs of scales. They were playful and always running around in their vivarium while Mirik crawled about in his smaller vivarium the few times he mustered enough energy to move.

It was heartbreaking.

Something was wrong, but I couldn't figure out what. His mother confused me. Every time I cared for her young—as was the case now—she would park herself at the closest glass edge of her vivarium to observe. You'd almost think she was longing for him. But the minute I brought him over to her, she hissed and displayed an aggressive behavior so that he wouldn't come closer to her and the others. When his siblings had attempted to approach him, she had chastised them and forced them back.

But why?!

Initially, I'd wondered if my scent on him had made her reject Mirik. But she didn't mind me holding any of her other babies and welcomed them back without a problem. Was it because he was the first successfully enhanced young? When he'd been born, she had fed him and looked after him just like the others. But, within three days, he had started showing clear signs of distress. She'd rejected him then and never allowed him back closer to the rest of them.

I didn't mind caring for the adorable little alien creature. If not for the scales, flatter nose, and large telescopic eyes, the Kirdie would look exactly like Earth's version of the mole. However, despite my best effort, we were losing the battle. Lily, the mother, was regularly licking her young, coating them with a substance that clearly hastened the thickening of their skin and development of their scales. I had tried to replicate that substance for Mirik, but I didn't know when to apply it or in what amount. She also seemed to be regurgitating something for her offspring at completely odd times and not for all of them. I was shooting blind.

I finished feeding Mirik and put him back in his own little vivarium by himself. He emitted a sad little keening sound that further broke my heart. The knock on the glass wall surrounding the lab startled me. I turned around to see Patty waving at me. My heart sank, already guessing what this one was about.

I raised one finger to indicate for her to hold on while I wrapped things up in the lab, then quickly exited into the antechamber where my work desk occupied the right side of the room, and Josie's took the left one. I pointed her to the small seating area with a well-used, beige loveseat, a matching chair, a massive bean bag where Josie and I often brainstormed ideas. The white board on the back wall covered in scribbles and formulas testified to it.

Patty settled in the chair, and I plopped myself on the beanbag.

"Sorry to bother you, I know you scientific-type are always busy," Patty said with an apologetic grin.

"No worries, I was wrapping up with the Kirdies," I said with a dismissive gesture. "Now, I have a million simulations to run, and I'm not really looking forward to it. So, any excuse to delay is welcomed."

She chuckled. "My sympathies. Math and I were never on friendly terms. I'm actually here about the Christmas party. I'm making plans for seating, food, activities, the whole shebang. I need a proper headcount. You'll be attending, right?"

I squirmed in my seat. As a proper introvert, my instinctive reaction whenever someone invited me somewhere was to look for an excuse not to go. It was super lame and completely irrational. Most of the time, when I actually forced myself to go out, I had a blast. Well, at least for the first couple of hours, and then the itch to leave and be back in the peace and quiet of my domicile came back with a vengeance. The problem was that every time you said yes, your host or event organizer always gave you an epic guilt trip the minute you wanted to leave. That made me even less inclined to show up in the first place.

But I also didn't want to spend Christmas alone.

"I don't know," I said, truthfully. "A part of me wants to, but—"

"You must!" Patty said, raising her palm in an arresting gesture. "There are too few people left on the base right now for you to deprive us of your presence. Also, there are four very eligible bachelors that would love to be your date."

"Oh please!" I said, rolling my eyes. "You already know I'm not going with Wilson. So, you can strike that one out."

She pursed her lips, visibly displeased. "There's Benny. He—"

"Oh my God! Seriously?" I exclaimed, flabbergasted. "I don't think Benny has used his shower more than twice in the three years he's been here. I also suspect he never figured out how to use his washing machine, or that he could use the laundry service on the base. I'd lick Pig-Pen's entire ass before I go on a date with Benny."

"Pig-Pen?" Patty asked, confused.

"A fictional character in a classic, old-school comic strip from Earth," I said dismissively. "Bottomline, the answer is hell no!"

"Okay, okay. I have been working with him on the hygiene issue," Patty conceded. "But he works alone in the engine room. If he had more social interaction, like with a girlfriend, I'm sure—"

One look at my face sufficed for her to understand it would be unwise to proceed further.

"There's Carl—"

"Who scratches his balls twenty-four seven and only stops long enough to bite his nails," I said, unimpressed. "Not to mention that a doorknob would provide a far more interesting conversation than he does."

"Fine. What about—?"

"Patty, save it," I interrupted in a severe tone. "Look, I understand you're trying to be helpful, but right now, you're not. I'm getting a little tired of everyone trying to dictate my personal life at every turn. I'm single, not desperate. My refusing to settle with the first bachelor to come sniff my way doesn't make me a prissy diva. And as the Personnel Coordinator, I'm giving you a heads up right now that I'm this close from filing a harassment complaint against Wilson."

Patty recoiled, her light green eyes widening in shock. "Harassment? Isn't that a bit much for some inoffensive flirting?"

"No, it's not. He's relentless despite me telling him repeatedly to piss off," I snapped. "The son of a bitch even had the nerve to put a Counselor on my ass!"

"He sent Antonia to pay you a visit?!" Patty asked, her eyes sparkling with delight at this juicy bit of gossip she'd been unaware of.

That did nothing to improve my mood.

"Yes," I snarled. "Two days after Worf had to threaten to bite that bubble ass of his so he would stop ringing my doorbell, Wilson called her saying I needed therapy. And that's not funny."

"Well, you are very closed off," Patty said carefully, while trying to hold back her visible urge to laugh. "Are you sure you don't need someone to talk to?"

"No, I don't!" I replied angrily. "The Dick simply refuses to understand that the only disposable douche that will ever go up my vagina is not called Wilson."

Patty gasped in shock. If I wasn't so pissed, I'd probably be shocked, too. It wasn't my style to be so crudely vulgar. She huffed and flicked her long, dark brown hair over her shoulder.

"And why are you so persistent with that idiot anyway? Did he put you up to this?" I asked, narrowing my eyes suspiciously at her.

She shrugged and pinched her thin lips. "He keeps begging for me to help win you over. And frankly, I think you could use a boyfriend. It can't be healthy for someone to be celibate for years like you have been."

"Patty, if the need to scratch an itch gets that bad, I'll just order a sex bot," I deadpanned. "Now, regarding the party, I'll have to think about it. But if I decide to come, you better not give me lip the minute I choose to leave, or I promise to make a really ugly scene."

"Fine, we can—"

My com rang, interrupting her. I picked it up only to be told by the shipping clerk at the docking bay that a huge package and a number of smaller ones had arrived for me. Due to their fragile nature, they would be delivered immediately.

"I have to go," I said to Patty as soon as I hung up, my voice bubbling with excitement. "I have some large packages being delivered. I guess my sex bot has arrived," I added with a wink.

She snorted and shook her head at me.

I headed straight home, kicked off my shoes and removed my bra, as per my usual routine. After a moment's hesitation, I decided to swap my more or less fitted blouse for one of my favorite oversized shirts. My leggings were the only hugging clothes I didn't mind wearing at home. They genuinely felt like a second skin, so much so I would forget I was even wearing them.

As I hadn't ordered anything, the packages could only be my Christmas gifts from Clarisse. However, the shipping clerk had mentioned some 'fragile' items. I'd asked my sister for clothes and a chew toy—hardly delicate material requiring immediate handling. It obviously had to be the surprise she'd promised. That, more than anything else had me buzzing with curiosity. I loved surprises. It could simply be a cheap candy necklace, I'd be ecstatic.

Naturally, I spent the next five minutes—which felt like ten times as much—waiting for the delivery guy to arrive while speculating on what it could be. Perishable items were usually frozen and kept in a temperature-controlled container, so I doubted it was that. Clarisse knew I didn't care for fancy, delicate decorations. So, not only she wouldn't send me something like that, but if she did, it would be padded with so many layers, only a nuke could damage it.

That left me with a living thing. I didn't do plants, but I loved pets. It had to be some awkward-looking alien critter that most people would find freakish. Knowing me, I'd fawn over how incredibly adorable it was. I could only hope it would get along with Worf. Thankfully, my sister was thorough enough that she would have done her homework on that front. Sensing my excitement, my little hellion was jumping all around me, making hooting sounds.

I almost squealed when the door finally rang and had to tell

Worf to calm down he was so hyper. You'd think the presents were for him. Well, if the chew toy was included, then he did have somewhat of a claim.

I opened the door to find Jules outside my door with a sheepish expression on his face, and a large hovercart carrying a few nicely wrapped boxes. He'd been avoiding deliveries at my place since he'd pulled that stunt with Wilson a week ago. Patty had certainly let him know I'd not appreciated the swap, although she likely described it as me having thrown a tantrum of epic proportions and warned him I'd skin him alive when next we met. Just a tiny bit exaggerated... The gangly beanpole of a delivery guy had probably been shaking in his boots the whole time.

He was a sweet guy. Like Patty, he always looked starved and like the first gust of wind would sweep him away. In her case, being a former model, she'd kept the habit of barely eating. But in his, he just had a crazy metabolism. Born of a Moroccan mother and an American father from Alabama, Jules's pronounced southern twang when he spoke clashed so much with his middle eastern looks that it always gave me whiplash.

I was opening my mouth to gently chastise him when I noticed a humongous hovering container that suspiciously resembled a stasis chamber. However, a reinforced, platinum lid casing prevented me from seeing inside. It screamed high quality and especially high security. Whatever it contained held tremendous value. What kind of extravagant expense had my sister done for me this time?

"You've received some interesting packages, Ms. Wright," Jules said, his embarrassment fading to be replaced by the oddest look in his dark brown eyes. "May I put them inside?"

I nodded, absentmindedly, too busy trying to figure out which company the elegant golden logo belonged to. It appeared to be a word written in stylized alien letters. My money said it came from Alpha Centauri. Whatever it was though, Worf appeared to approve. He kept running around the elliptical container and trying to 'boop' it with his forehead.

Jules unloaded the boxes from the hovercart, piling them up near the couch in the living room. I moved the coffee table out of the way so that the chamber could hover to that location instead before Jules set it down. He handed me a small pamphlet with instructions on operating the chamber. After one last strange glance at it, he looked back at me with an odd mix of amusement, disbelief, and confusion. You'd think I'd done something shockingly out of character, or flat out inappropriate.

"*Enjoy*, Ms. Wright," Jules said before leaving.

That, too, held an underlying meaning that had me even more confused.

I locked the door and went back inside my living room. A quick look at the pamphlet indicated a twelve-digit code was required to open the chamber, and the wretched thing wasn't included. I called my sister on vidcom, heedless of the steep cost it would be should I run out of minutes. I suspected it had been a deliberate request on her part to make sure I wouldn't open it without her witnessing it.

While waiting for the call to connect, I started opening the other boxes. Started being the operative word here as Worf took over with a speed and savagery that left me speechless. Like a scaly ball full of claws and teeth, he bounced around shredding the wrapping paper and slicing the boxes open with a rather scary surgical precision. He stopped as suddenly as he'd started, standing proudly on his stunted legs, puffing out his round belly, and grinning at me while waiting to be congratulated. Despite the mess, my little Fudian had effectively opened my presents without damaging the contents.

I burst out laughing at the sight of a life-size, brown foot, the same color as my complexion, and made in a squeezable material. The massive big toe looked like it had been stung by a swarm of bees. An extendable stick could also be inserted in a small opening in the ankle should I want to tease Worf with it. I chuckled while my little brat began chewing on it then tried calling my sister again when the first attempt failed to connect.

After quickly picking up the mess Worf had made, I moved on to browsing through and trying out the gorgeous large shirts and sundresses my sister had sent me. They were far more fashionable than what I would have bought for myself. The exquisite fabric fell just right on me, making me look slender instead of lost in a potato sack as was often the case with the stuff I bought myself. Every piece, especially the dresses, were chic enough that I could go to work or even to parties wearing them.

I was almost done sorting out the clothes when the call finally connected.

"Dang, woman! Was about time!" I exclaimed when Clarisse's pretty face appeared on the screen. "I've been calling you forever!"

"Hello to you, too, sis," Clarisse replied with a haughty expression. "Some of us have strict work schedules they must stick to."

"Some of us were smart and chose a job with far more flexible schedules," I deadpanned.

"You're just a non-conformist. One who looks sexy as hell in a certain dress, I might add," she said smugly.

I glanced down at myself and grinned. The sleeveless white muumuu with beautiful black, red, and gold tribal patterns, especially around the hem, was absolutely gorgeous. The fancy-looking, but sturdy fabric fell to my ankles and was as soft as a baby's bum.

"I'll admit, for a stiff conformist, your fashion tastes are spot on. I love every single garment you sent me!" I said in all sincerity. I *hated* shopping for clothes. "You have my permission to continue sending me clothes whenever you feel like it."

She snorted. "Normally, I should flip you the bird, but I believe I'm going to take you up on that offer."

I grinned then cast a meaningful glance at the chamber. "What the heck is that? And why did the delivery guy give me a funky look when he brought it? You know we have strict restrictions as far as the type of exotic pets we can have on the base, right?"

Clarisse's face heated, and the sudden uncertain expression on her face raised a billion red flags. My sister never second-guessed herself. At times, her confidence bordered arrogance. And yet, the wretch was indeed usually right in whatever call she made.

"No worries, nothing within it breaks any regulations. I've handled all the legal registrations and paperwork. You only need to confirm and approve your intention of keeping him within fourteen days," my sister said carefully.

"Him? So, it is a pet?" I asked, dying with curiosity. "Come on, woman, spill the beans! And give me that damn code!"

She chewed her bottom lip, hesitating. I lifted my palms facing up in a questioning fashion as she seemed to struggle on how to respond.

"Look, don't freak out and keep an open mind, okay?" Clarisse finally said, more nervous than I'd ever seen her in my entire life. "I moved mountains to make this happen because I really, *really* think this is the *best* gift I could ever give you. Just give it a chance, all right?"

"Clarisse," I said in a warning tone, although worry was starting to take root in the pit of my stomach.

"The code is Pi," she said, looking almost defeated.

For a second, I thought she meant a meat or fruit pie, which made no sense whatsoever, before realizing she meant the number Pi. I plugged in the twelve first digits of the mathematical constant on the discreet interface on top of the chamber. Its edges lit up, and it unlocked with a soft hiss. Worf stopped chewing the artificial toe to stare at the chamber with the same look of wonder and curiosity that was undoubtedly etched on my face.

The invisible seam of the lid split open right in the middle, each half retracting into the side of the chamber. Worf emitted a single whoop as I stood transfixed at the sight of the gorgeous —and utterly naked—man lying unconscious in the chamber. My sister spoke, but her words didn't compute. My brain had tilted.

I couldn't tell how long I stood there just staring at him before looking up at the screen. My sister appeared to hold a breath while waiting for me to say something.

"There's an unconscious naked guy in my living room who looks just like Sean Novak but with a Klingon's forehead," I said, numbly. "I can't believe you gifted me a sex bot! No fucking wonder Jules was looking at me funny. And I just told Patty I had ordered one. Oh my God!"

I pressed my hands on my burning cheeks and let myself drop on my couch, winded.

"Hey, it's not so bad," my sister said, trying to sound cheerful despite her obvious uncertainty. "I mean, you love Sean. You've seen everything he's ever done. Don't tell me you haven't fantasized about banging him!"

I gaped at her in disbelief. "Fantasizing about banging an A-list actor, and getting a life size, fancy sex bot looking like him are two completely different things!" I exclaimed. "People are going to think I'm some kind of stalker-pervert or something!"

"He's not an identical replica of Sean, just has similarities," Clarisse argued. "They could almost pass as siblings, except for his crown."

"His crown?" I asked, my brain still trying to parse through the mess of emotions coursing through me.

"Yeah, the bone ridges on his forehead," she explained. "It's called a crown."

"Right," I said, looking back at the hot stud lying in the

chamber. "Clare, I can't… What the heck do you want me to do with it?"

"Bone him?" she said as if the answer was self-evident.

"A sex bot, Clarisse?! Really? Do you think I'm THAT desperate?" I asked, looking at her gobsmacked.

"A sex bot beats sex toys. And don't even try to make me believe you don't have a stash of those," she said, making a face that dared me to deny it.

I scrunched my face, my cheeks heating some more.

"I mean, come on Kitty-Kat," Clarisse said in an encouraging tone. "Don't you think a sex toy that does all the work for you is much better? Plus, Anders—that's his name—is already at your place. He will give you guaranteed orgasms—note the plural here—every single time. Best of all, you don't have to clean and take care of him when you're done getting your rocks off because he performs self-maintenance. Seriously, what more could you want? And be honest, don't you want to bang him?"

This time, even my ears felt on fire. "All right, fine. All of the above does sound good," I admitted reluctantly, still wishing the floor would open beneath me and swallow me whole. "But still, shagging an android feels pretty damn desperate."

"Then, it's a good thing that he's not an android," Clarisse deadpanned.

"WHAT?!"

"Just so you know, this gift is non-refundable," Clarisse said quickly. "You'll find all the instructions in the pouch next to his head. Oh my, look at the time! I have another meeting. Enjoy your gift. Love you! Bye!"

I gaped at the dark screen as my sister ended the call. Snapping out of my shock, I called back. As expected, the wuss didn't answer.

What the fuck did she mean by he wasn't an android? Had she bought me some sort of sex slave? She wouldn't be that crazy. Not only was it illegal in the Solar System, but she knew I wouldn't be down with that shit. In truth, she wouldn't be okay with that either. So, what the heck was he?

I carefully poked his arm. The skin felt exactly like a human's and was warm to the touch. His lack of reaction prompted me to poke him again a bit more forcefully, without any response. Yeah, Anders was absurdly hot. I wanted pretty badly to cop a feel. Had Clarisse not told me he wasn't a droid, my hands would have gone grabby something fierce. Even now, I had to force myself not to stare at his cock, quite impressive even limp. Strangely enough, the thought that Clarisse might have seen him naked both displeased and embarrassed me.

Heaving a sigh, I picked up the instruction pouch which had another code redeemable on the Universal Streaming Network. I entered the code and sat down to watch the most unbelievable introduction to the 'personal gift' I had just received.

CHAPTER 5
ANDERS

The first spark of consciousness drew me out of stasis. Confusion and conflicting emotions wafted to me: distress, excitement, humiliation, and arousal mingled and battled each other. In the background, Jarak's voice was speaking, explaining what I was. But I couldn't focus on his words. The most wonderful spiritual energy swirled around me. Its source: Kathleen's aura. My entire being raged with the need to claim her. Even that human vessel responded to her beauty.

My eyelids fluttered open. The dim lights in the room felt gentle on my eyes as I looked up at Kathleen. She looked lovely in the white, sleeveless summer dress she was wearing. Her light-brown eyes glued to the screen, she was chewing her bottom lip while twisting a lock of her shoulder-length, reddish-brown curly hair.

My human vessel responded again at laying eyes on the source of such a beautiful aura. I had been so worried about traveling to a strange planetary system with a species so few of us had any experience with. But feeling her soul now, I knew beyond any doubt that I had found my mate. However, her emotions clearly broadcast she didn't know how to handle me.

Based on what I was hearing from the video, Jarak still had another five minutes to go. I debated whether to wait until he was done to inform Kathleen that I had awakened. Just as the thought crossed my mind, a green ball of scales jumped inside the stasis chamber and landed on my stomach. I immediately recognized Worf, the pesky critter that had chewed on Kathleen's toe. He hooted then grinned his gums at me.

"Worf!" Kathleen exclaimed, getting up to pull him off me. "You can't jump on him like... Oh, God! You're awake!"

She recoiled and took a few steps back, clutching the little Fudian to her chest.

"Do not be afraid, Kathleen," I said in a soothing voice. "I can never harm you."

I sat in the chamber before getting up on my feet. I was one head taller than her; the perfect height for the perfect hugs. From all the research I had done on humans, females often buried their faces in their mate's neck. I wanted to feel that with Kathleen, how her curly hair would tickle my skin, and her breath would fan on my chest.

Kathleen's gaze roamed over me with an odd mix of awe, arousal, and horror. The latter seriously threw me for a loop.

"You're naked," she said, as if she thought I wasn't aware of it.

"Indeed," I replied, uncertain how to respond.

"You need to cover yourself! Why did they send you naked?" she asked.

My heart sank upon hearing those words.

"Do you... Do you not like my appearance? If so, I apologize. I didn't have specific details as to your preferences. So, I improvised—"

"Oh no! You're fine! I mean, you're *very fine*!" Kathleen interrupted, her gaze involuntarily roaming over me. Her undeniable attraction soothed my blossoming distress about my appearance. "But... You know..." She cleared her throat. "You shouldn't be naked in front of strangers."

"The Seekers usually like seeing their Lyrian naked so that they can admire the final result of their wish in the flesh. Many also want to mate with him right away to have offspring quickly," I explained.

The mortified expression on her face made me want to laugh. The strange mix of her conflicting emotions was quite intriguing. She was outraged on our behalf, and yet, that thought had aroused her, and she even empathized with the Seekers.

"Doesn't that... bother you?" she asked, slightly confused.

"What? That our Seeker would want to bed us right away?" I asked.

She nodded.

"Not at all, quite the opposite," I answered sincerely. "We look forward to forming a deeper bond with our partner. As Empaths, the emotions of our partner are almost like a drug to us. Few moments are as powerful emotionally than during intimacy."

"Really?" Kathleen asked, putting down Worf who had been wiggling in her arms to be released. "You wouldn't mind if I just dragged you into my bedroom right this minute to have my way with you?" she challenged.

"Mind?" I repeated with a chuckle. "I would like that very much."

To my surprise, my voice had lowered, taking on a deeper tone with a will of its own as I pronounced those words. Kathleen's coppery skin erupted in goosebumps in response. My brain immediately registered that deep voices elicited a pleasure response in my partner. Simultaneously, a very pleasant heat blossomed in my nether region. Pictures of Kathleen naked in my arms, her hands roaming over me as I pushed myself inside her flashed through my mind.

To my dismay, blood rushed to my groin, engorging my phallus that began to rise. I had no problem letting her know she aroused me, but now didn't seem like an appropriate time.

"Oh, God!" Kathleen exclaimed as she witnessed my erection.

She turned on her heels and rushed inside a room adjacent to the living area. By the small glimpse I got inside the room from my current position, I presumed it to be a bedroom. She came back seconds later with a blue blanket, which she unfolded and extended to me. I took it, amused by her efforts not to look while her emotions screamed how turned on she was.

"Thank you," I said, wrapping the fabric around me. It still tented in front of me, which made me want to chuckle, but that seemed to help alleviate some of Kathleen's embarrassment. "I apologize for this. It seems that certain functions of the human body cannot be controlled unlike with most other species in Alpha Centauri."

"Controlled how?" Kathleen asked, genuinely curious. "Like telling your big boy to stay down?"

This time, I didn't refrain from laughing. "Big boy? Not too big, I hope?" I asked, immediately kicking myself for it.

I was truly curious about how satisfied she was with this body, or if I should go back to the drawing board. But making her comfortable with me was more important. I didn't want her thinking I was some sort of pervert. To my utter surprise—and total delight—she actually answered.

"Nope, not too big. Your overall concept," she said, gesturing at me, "was totally spot on. You're super-hot."

My cheeks and chest suddenly felt quite warm. From studying humans on my way here, I recognized the signs of blushing. It was unusual but not unpleasant. And above all, Kathleen's approval further increased my sense of well-being.

"Good, I am glad," I said humbly. "And to answer your question, yes, most Alpha Centauri species—both males and females—are able to control their reproductive organs. In some cultures, me showing my arousal without you giving your express consent and interest in copulating would have gotten me castrated."

"Oh, ouch!" Kathleen said, cringing.

"Ouch, indeed," I replied with a smile, more delighted than ever by her personality.

"Right, well, you might as well have a seat," she said, suddenly appearing slightly overwhelmed. "Are you thirsty? Hungry?"

"Not hungry, but a glass of water or a sweet drink would be welcomed," I said, before gladly taking a seat on her three-cushion couch.

Kathleen went to fetch the drink in the adjoining kitchen of the open concept living unit. The place was spacious, with light colors that created a soothing environment. To my surprise, the décor was fairly minimalist, her wall decorations being mostly limited to family pictures. The reading nook in the living area had a huge, plushy cushion that reminded me of a beanbag, but long enough to qualify as a chaise lounge. Kathleen's silhouette imprinted in the fluffy cushion on top testified she frequently used it.

She returned with a hover tray which she left hovering next to me in lieu of the coffee table she'd pushed to the corner to make room for my chamber. A glass of water, a jug of sweet iced tea, and an extra empty glass should I decide to go for the tea instead all sat on top of the tray. Holding a glass of iced tea in her hand, Kathleen went to take a seat in the chair rather than joining me on the couch. Although disappointed, I understood her reservations.

I downed the glass of water in one go, realizing how parched I'd actually been, before pouring myself some iced tea.

"Thank you," I said, with gratitude.

"Do you want more water?" she asked.

I shook my head. "No, I'm good now. Thank you," I replied sincerely.

A slightly uncomfortable silence settled between us. I wanted to talk more, but I could sense her trying to sort out her emotions and figuring out where to go from here. I felt at a total loss as to how to handle this situation. Lyrians were highly sought after in Alpha Centauri. None of my brothers had ever been in a situation like mine. It wasn't a pleasant feeling to have your partner unsure if she actually wanted to be with you.

"So… What are you?" Kathleen asked at last. "I mean, you're a Lyrian, but what is that exactly? You chose your appearance according to your interpretation of my tastes. Are you like a brain put inside a synthetic body?"

I burst out laughing. "No, all of this is me," I said gesturing at my body. "Lyrians are shifters. We can take whatever appearance we want and become whatever species our Seeker desires. Once we bond, that appearance becomes permanent. We inherit all the traits of that species, including any abilities or limitations."

"Oh wow! That's super cool!" she exclaimed with sincerity.

"It is," I said with a nod before smiling at Worf who was frantically chewing on some sort of fake foot.

"Aren't you afraid of being picked by someone you might not like?" Kathleen asked. "What if you realize I'm a total bitch, and you can't stand me? Or what if you do like me, but I can't stand you?"

"The Seeker doesn't choose us," I explained gently. "*We* choose *them*. They go through a thorough psychological evaluation, personality tests, and fill endless forms to be matched with one of us. Those potential matches review the Seeker's file to see if they are interested. If yes, they will test the Seeker's aura to confirm if they are indeed a match. In your case, it wasn't possible. But what information your sister provided made me like you enough to take the risk of coming here even without the certainty that I would like you. As for a Seeker realizing they don't like us, that has never happened. We are Empaths. All of our actions aim to please our partner. We thrive on it."

A powerful emotion ran through Kathleen. She hugged her glass to her chest while giving me a strange look. My words had deeply moved her. I realized then that my partner had low self-esteem. She didn't think anyone could be drawn enough to her to travel to a new planetary system on a whim, just to be with her. I would need to rectify that.

"You guys can see auras?" she asked.

"No. We do not see them. We feel them," I corrected. "It's like the spiritual energy that emanates from you. Have you ever felt naturally drawn to someone, not in a sexual way? Someone you just feel good being around them?"

"Yes," Kathleen conceded with a nod. "Not often, because I'm mostly antisocial," she added with an embarrassed chuckle. "But yes, there are some people I just instantly clicked with and enjoy being in their company, even if neither of us is talking."

"It's their aura," I replied with a smile. "It aligns with yours. I had hoped that our auras would be compatible."

"And?" Kathleen asked, a sliver of tension in her voice.

"My earlier physical reaction should tell you," I said teasingly, enjoying seeing her blush again. "Your aura is the most wonderful thing I have ever felt. I want to wrap myself in it, drown in it. I'd been afraid coming here that you wouldn't be who I had sensed in those quirky videos. But now, I know beyond any doubt that you're my soulmate."

"Sheesh," she said, once more embarrassed but deeply touched. "You sure know how to make a girl feel good about herself."

"Not *a* girl, just you," I replied.

She rubbed her nape and chewed her bottom lip. Her hesitations were wavering, but she still held on to some uncertainties.

"Everything you're saying is most definitely tempting,"

Kathleen admitted. "You're gorgeous, and you're apparently really drawn to me. However, I don't know you, and I'm not an Empath. Although I have a guest room, what if I'm not comfortable with you staying in my living unit?"

My back stiffened. It was a fair question; one we had already anticipated. However, it still hurt that she would consider sending me away.

"It would be very awkward and distressing for me, but your happiness is primordial," I answered in a measured tone. "I have sufficient credits to rent a guest room on the station."

"Why distressing?" Kathleen asked, tilting her head to the side.

"I need to bond with my chosen—with you," I replied. "Interactions with others cement my personality. But to ensure it is best aligned with my mate, as much as possible, social contact should be limited to her for the first couple of weeks. Why do you think I came here in stasis rather than as a passenger aboard the flight here?"

"Mingling with the other passengers would have affected your personality?" Kathleen asked, flabbergasted.

"Yes," I said with a nod. "It would have tainted my perceptions of good and bad, ugly and pretty, nice or mean, and general reaction to various things. For example, things you find funny or pleasant will also become that way for me. Why? Because they give you pleasure, which in turns also gives me pleasure. I derive my happiness from yours. In truth, an Empath bending over backwards to please his partner is self-serving."

She slightly frowned while reflecting on my words.

"Don't you have personal preferences?" she asked.

I chuckled. "Of course, we do. We're not blank canvases. That's why we must be matched with Seekers with personalities aligned with ours," I explained. "But you could say that we are incomplete. Lyrian males—who represent 85% of our population —live normal lives until puberty. During those early years, we develop our individual personalities. At that point, our basic Empathic abilities develop into their full spectrum. That's when we go into stasis to avoid being influenced by external forces."

"Oh my God! You spend your entire life in a chamber and hope to be matched?" Kathleen exclaimed, horrified.

"It's not that bad," I said, laughing. "It's a partial stasis during which we learn all the things that have piqued our interest based on our personalities. Thanks to that, I fluently speak eighty-three languages, know over a hundred different combat techniques, master mathematics, physics, chemistry, as well as the culture and history of all sentient species in Alpha Centauri, to name a few."

"Whoa…" Kathleen whispered, floored. "You're going to find me super boring then."

"Absolutely not," I said, shaking my head vigorously. "Everything about you fascinates me. Not only you, the individual, but also the human species as a whole since I knew nothing other than that you populated the Solar System. Becoming the perfect partner for you while discovering and cementing my adult personality, as a human no less, is a thrilling prospect."

She looked at me with confusion and awe. "You're really serious about wanting to just please me in every way, aren't you?"

"Absolutely," I said with conviction. "Lyrians thrive on their partner's emotions. My happiness depends entirely on yours. So, naturally, I will do everything in my power to make sure you are."

"You drive a hard bargain," Kathleen mumbled.

I smiled, my chest warming with a pleasant feeling as she finally came to terms with my presence and accepted to keep me —at least for the time being. The war was far from won, but I welcomed this first victory.

She rolled her shoulders and stretched her neck.

"Do you want a massage?" I offered.

"What?" Kathleen exclaimed.

"You are tense, and your back muscles pain you," I said. "I have trained in over 129 different forms of massages. I would be happy to give you a different type every day, or even two a day if you wish."

Kathleen's eyes sparked with envy, that she immediately clamped down before eyeing me suspiciously. "You want to give me a massage while having a raging hard on?"

I recoiled before casting a glance at my groin and then looking back at her. "I'm sorry. I believe I will remain hard for a while. My body is very drawn to yours," I said sheepishly. "However, while I may not control some of its functions, my body does not control *me*. I *will* behave. Remember that upsetting you upsets me. Eighty-four of those massages are non-sexual. It will do you good!"

She chewed her bottom lip, fighting to hang on to the last shreds of her hesitation. "But... Doesn't it bother you to be this hard? Won't massaging me make it worse?"

"No," I said sincerely. "Obviously, I want you, but the wait makes me anticipate even more our first time together. I've waited my whole life to meet the female who would stir such a response from me. So, I cannot possibly regret feeling its manifestation, at long last."

"Damn, you're good," Kathleen whispered, almost begrudgingly. And yet, she was pleased. She squirmed on her seat before coming to a decision. "Okay. I could use a good massage. I don't have a massage table, but I can replicate one."

"That would be wonderful," I said with a grin, my palms already itching with the need to touch her. "While you do that, maybe you can indicate where I could put away my chamber, and unpack my things?"

"Your things?" she asked, confused.

"There's a fairly large storage compartment under the chamber," I explained. "Although I arrived naked, I do have some clothes with me."

"Oh, right! Good. Hmmm… This way," Kathleen said, getting up.

I followed.

CHAPTER 6
KATHLEEN

My mind was reeling, while my ovaries were doing backflips. As I led him to the guest room, I cast a discreet glance at my chest. As I feared, my freaking nipples had gone into attention whore mode, poking their heads through my loose shirt. Anders was soooooooo fucking hot. To think he wanted to roll in the hay with me, right here, right now. And that spectacular hard on of his made it no secret.

And that cock? Holy mackerel on a cracker!

My already drenched undies felt a wee bit wetter as I began throbbing inside. Clarisse was right—yet again. No collection of battery-operated boyfriends could rival the real thing, especially when said thing looked like a Greek god, was hung like a horse, and determined to give me enough orgasms to make me speak in tongues. So, why the fuck was I bringing him to my guest room —a very messy one at that—instead of dragging him to my bedroom and riding that glorious cock of his until it fell off?

Because my so-called non-conformist ass is still very much conformist.

There was nothing wrong with two consenting adults banging on day one. But it seemed I wasn't so open as to play hide the snake in the cave within five minutes of meeting a well-hung hunk. Okay, it had been at least half an hour, but that was still too fast.

And yet, here you are about to let him rub his hands all over your naked body, you ho!

Hey! I've had plenty of complete strangers giving me massages in spas. Nothing wrong with getting one from a hot alien stud who believed me to be his soulmate.

I opened the door to the guest room and cringed. As I never had guests, it had pretty much turned into the 'here's-an-open-spot-to-dump-this-random-shit-in' room.

"I'm really sorry about the mess," I said, mortified. "I had not expected a visitor, or all of this shit would have been cleaned up. Half of this crap I mean to throw out."

I hurried to move a bunch of old printed reports and files from the bed, as well as a couple of boxes containing who knew what. I pushed aside an old broken chair I'd been planning on fixing forever. A number of gadgets I had replicated, but that never quite properly worked, cluttered the little space between the empty dresser and the treadmill I had used a total of three times—go me!

"Stop fretting, Kathleen," Anders said in an amused voice. "I can handle it. I'll sort everything out, and you can show me what you want thrown out afterward. After so much time in stasis, my body can definitely use the exercise."

"But you're my guest! It's not for you to—"

"Please, Kathleen. Let me," he said, interrupting me. "I really want to do this for you. And it will give me a chance to set up my room in a way that's efficient for me."

I scrunched my face and gave him a 'what the fuck' look. "You know, you're the first person I've ever met who is this eager to clean up someone's mess without getting paid for it."

"Your mess is *my* mess, Kathleen. And pleasing you is extremely enjoyable," Anders countered.

The way his voice dropped saying that had my girly bits standing at attention again.

"If you're trying to make me keep you, you're doing a damn good job of it," I mumbled, feeling slightly annoyed and totally smitten, especially since he seemed genuine in his request.

"I'm pleased to hear it," Anders said, puffing out that lickable, muscular chest of his.

And those perky nipples… I wanted to make 'meep-meep' noises while pinching them.

"At least, let me change the bedding for you," I offered, feeling like the worst hostess in mankind's history. My mom would disown me if she knew.

"You can bring me the new sheets, and I'll make the bed with them," Anders said with a shameless grin on his face.

I instinctively knew there would be no point arguing with him. But did I really want to? I hated cleaning and changing the bedding—among a fairly long list of other chores I always procrastinated about. If doing them made him happy, who was I to deny him the pleasure?

You shameless, lazy ass.

Yep, that was my middle-name. I'd make it up to him later.

"All right, then. I'll be right back," I conceded.

He gave me a panty-melting smile that made my brain tilt again. I turned around to go fetch the fresh linens and almost stepped on Worf spying on us while chewing that artificial foot. He stepped out of the way in extremis with an offended hoot and glared at me.

"Sorry, pumpkin," I said, mortified, before casting an embarrassed look over my shoulder at Anders.

His smile broadened, but he didn't say a word. He reminded me of a Roman Emperor with the blanket wrapped around his waist and the bone ridges on his forehead that served as his crown. He probably thought me a clumsy goof.

That wouldn't be a first.

I chose my fanciest set of blankets, grabbed a couple of towels and a toothbrush, which I brought over to him. He'd already stripped the bed of its old bedding and moved enough things littering the room to free a nice spot for his chamber.

"There you go," I said, handing him the little package.

"Thank you, Kathleen," Anders said with that strange Mona Lisa smile of his.

I would have given anything to know what thoughts were currently crossing his mind. It was all the more embarrassing that, as an Empath, he undoubtedly knew just how much he was turning me on. Being with someone who always knew how I felt would take some getting used to.

I nodded then left him to go create the massage table. The large replicator resembled a 3D printer with a series of pre-programmed common objects. I tapped the interface and accessed the pattern store to look for one of their best massage table models. A couple more taps sufficed to purchase and down-load it. The replicator immediately went to work. It would take nearly thirty minutes for it to finish printing. In the meantime, I would seize the opportunity to take a quick shower.

Although I had already taken one this morning, having been celibate for the past three years, I hadn't exactly been too rigorous with my shaving routine. My pits I had gotten perma-nently shaved with laser hair removal, but I'd been too self-conscious to have it done for my pubic hair. As a biracial woman, I'd been lucky enough to take after my father's black genetics, which meant fairly little body hair. I hadn't shaved my legs in years and frankly still couldn't see any hair to remove. However, my hoo-hah could use a trim. I wasn't planning on jumping onto the naughty list just yet, but better be prepared for anything.

I made quick work of it, while cycling through the endless arguments justifying why I couldn't just fully enjoy my present. In the same breath, I wondered at the madness of letting this complete stranger—alien no less—move in with me. Granted, Clarisse would have never sent him to me if there was the remotest risk to my welfare, but it was still weird and reckless, even for me.

After wrapping a huge towel around me, with still a few more minutes left before the table was done printing, I did a quick search on Lyrians, especially for warnings. To my delight, I found none; quite the opposite. Every single article stated instead that in Alpha Centauri, it was a privilege and mark of status to be chosen by one of them. The best part? Divorces, separations, or failed relationships involving them were nil.

The beep of the replicator completing its tasks forced me away from the computer. I picked up a couple more towels and stepped into the hallway to find Anders playing with Worf. Barefoot but wearing skin-tight black shorts that hid nothing of the scrumptious curve of his butt, and a see-through, off-white shirt that hugged every chiseled muscle of his abs, my alien gift was illegally sexy.

My heart melted seeing him play toe-toss with my little Fudian. Standing in the middle of the living room, Anders allowed Worf to latch onto his toe with his mouth. He then waved his foot back and forth, with my little green menace hanging on, before tossing his foot forward. I couldn't tell if Worf lost his grip or deliberately let go—I suspected the latter—but he would fly backward and make a backflip. As soon as he flawlessly landed on his stunted legs, my pet would run right back to bite Anders's toe again. The affectionate expression on the Lyrian's face as he looked at my little baby, and his amused chuckles as he genuinely seemed to enjoy playing that silly game with him, had tears pricking my eyes.

Worf had a rough start in life. He'd already been severely injured by his pack by the time I'd rescued him. After that, it took a long time for him to come out of his shell. Obviously, I wasn't his mother, but he was still like my baby to me, and he loved me unconditionally. He was usually shy with strangers, unless he believed they were a threat to me, and then he'd go feral on them. Any man I would ever consider entering into a relationship with would need to get along with Worf. Therefore, to see the two of them hit it off so quickly got me even more excited about exploring this further.

Just as Worf was running back for another round, Anders's head suddenly jerked towards me, as if he'd sensed my presence. His amused expression shifted into one of such tenderness and happiness that I all but melted into a puddle. Damn, that man knew just how to make a girl feel like a flipping goddess.

"I believe it's ready," I said timidly.

"Wonderful," he said with a grin, shaking Worf off his foot. "Let me get it for you. I figured the best spot was in the living room. I've taken the liberty of moving some of the furniture, if that's okay."

"It's perfect," I said, impressed with his logistics.

Where I'd haphazardly moved the coffee table out of the way earlier to make room for his chamber, he'd properly placed it against the wall, and the chair next to it. All the clothes Clarisse had sent me were neatly folded on top of the coffee table. Damn, that guy was definitely a keeper.

"Great," he said, pleased by my reaction.

Anders entered the small den that should have been my office but served as another storage room on top of containing the large replicator. He picked up the table like it weighed nothing and carried it to the living room. The beauty of replicators instead of 3D printers was their ability to recreate all types of materials, even cushiony ones, and sparing us the trouble of cleaning the rough edges afterward.

I felt a little self-conscious as Anders helped me lie down on my stomach on the table and fit my face in the hole. I unwrapped the towel and let him take it away from me. As much as it embarrassed me to be lying down in my granny panties, it felt better than being completely naked with only the towel covering my ass.

My pulse picked up as his incredibly soft hands adjusted my position on the table. It had been too long since I'd found myself in such a state of undress in front of a man who wasn't a medical doctor. Anticipation, arousal, and a great deal of trepidation had my blood pumping in my veins.

I lifted my head at the sound of a container opening, but Anders tsked me back down into my relaxed position.

"These are Lyrian beads that I will place on you. They diffuse a soothing heat that you should find quite agreeable," Anders said in a soft voice that gave me goosebumps.

However, he didn't put them on me immediately. From the sound, he appeared to place the container on the table, close to my head. A slight popping sound followed before the most delicious aroma wafted to me. I couldn't quite describe it. Flowery or fruity wouldn't apply, and yet it was light, fresh, airy, and somewhat sweet. The sound of Anders's hands rubbing against each other lasted only a few seconds before the searing heat of his palms settled on my back.

I never expected the loud moan that spilled out of my mouth as soon as he began rubbing the oil into my back. My skin tingled, and my muscles seemed to heave a major sigh of relief as if the weight of the world had suddenly been lifted from me. Anders chuckled softly with a smugness that could have been annoying if I wasn't literally melting under his touch. I didn't even care about Worf hooting, while my toes were curling.

He applied the oil on my back, my neck, and my arms before stopping. I felt so damn languid, I barely had the strength to whimper in protest.

He chuckled again. "Patience, love. I'm only getting started," Anders said.

That pleased me tremendously.

My Lyrian then proceeded to apply the gems he had previously mentioned. They didn't actually feel like stones, but rather like coin-shaped patches that he applied at specific spots on my back, nape, and my arms. I suspected the placement matched their version of some kind of acupuncture points. They immediately began to infuse me with a pleasant heat that penetrated all the way to my bones.

Anders moved on to repeat the process with my legs. By the time he was done, I was a drooling mess. And then he proceeded to massage me again over the beads. They were so thin, I barely even felt them as his hands roamed over me. My nerve endings had become so sensitive, each movement of his palms all but provoked micro-orgasms on their path. This may not have been a sexual massage—and I was much too languid to be aroused—but it might as well have been. It was *that* good.

When he finally stopped and began removing the beads, I was too comatose to move. Anders put the towel over me and carefully rolled me to the side, covering me at the same time before picking me up in his arms. I buried my face in his neck. His arms tightened around me, and he carried me to the couch before sitting down and settling me on his lap. I snuggled against him while he gently caressed my hair and my back. I couldn't tell if I fell asleep, but I'd never felt so relaxed, so wonderful, and so safe. For the next little while, time lost all meaning while I reveled in this sense of well-being, cocooned in his warm embrace.

The first signs of hunger eventually pulled me out of my semi-torpor. I opened my eyes to find Worf curled up on my lap, napping. Still feeling a little groggy, I lifted my head to look at Anders. He smiled at me, looking utterly content and happy. Damn, the man was perfect.

"Did I fall asleep?" I asked, my words a little slurred.

"Maybe," he said with a grin.

"Sorry," I said, scrunching my face.

"Don't be," he argued. "That's the greatest compliment you could give me. It proves I did my work correctly."

"You did it beyond correctly. That was amazing. You can do that to me anytime you want," I retorted, still feeling like I was floating on a cloud.

"Remember you said that," he replied. "I very much intend to take you up on that offer. But for now, I can feel your growing hunger. I can prepare dinner while you get dressed."

"Oh no! You're my guest," I said, straightening on his lap. "I'm the one that should be preparing a meal for you."

"I'm your 'unexpected' partner who happens to love the opportunity to take care of you," he deadpanned. "But I also want to show you why, even though you didn't ask for me, you should keep me forever."

"You really want us to work out," I said, once again baffled he would want me.

"I'm crazy about your aura, about you," Anders said with a conviction that turned me upside down, while brushing aside a lock of my hair on my forehead. "Even when you were sleeping, I've never felt so fulfilled. I could have stayed like this forever, just holding you in my arms. You were made for me."

"You're really growing on me," I said.

"Good," he said with a happy grin. He gently lifted Worf from my lap then laid him down on the cushion next to us before getting up, still holding me. He carefully let me down, making sure I was steady enough on my feet. "Now, go get dressed. I'll see what I can whip up for us."

"Okay, but I must warn you there isn't much in the fridge or the pantry," I said sheepishly.

"Don't worry, I'll work something out," Anders replied with confidence.

"All right. Don't feel bad if it's too hopeless," I said, embarrassed. "Worst case scenario, we'll order in."

He nodded. I tightened my towel around me and made my

way to my bedroom. Initially, I'd both hoped and feared he'd get frisky during that massage, but I couldn't be happier about how it had turned out in the end. Anders was fucking wonderful. Whatever reservations I still had about being gifted a 'mail-in' groom, that man was a keeper. I could only pray that once the honeymoon phase ended, I'd still feel the same about him, because I was falling hard and fast for my alien.

CHAPTER 7
ANDERS

For years, as a Fledgling, I'd feared what meeting my mate would be like, I'd been terrified of losing myself into the personality and likes of another. But now, I just wanted to endlessly bask in Kathleen's aura. She was breathtakingly beautiful. My arms ached to hold her again. She had felt so delicate, fragile, and trusting in her sleep. I hated that we'd be sleeping in separate rooms. It wasn't about sex, although I also looked forward to that. I just loved being infused by her aura while my arms were wrapped around her body—making us almost become one.

I opened the fridge, and my jaw dropped at its barren state. The pantry was just as pathetic. My woman had not been kidding by saying there wasn't much. Although not a big fan of canned food, I decided to use the crab meat from one of the cupboards to make some crab cakes. The handful of fairly tired regular and sweet potatoes on their last leg in the fridge would be tasty once mashed, and a surprisingly fresh head of lettuce and cherry tomatoes would make a nice side salad. Although Kathleen had some vinaigrette in the fridge, I decided to make my own since my mate at least had a very respectable selection of spices.

Kathleen returned while I was peeling the potatoes and offered to help, which I obviously refused.

"I may be in full courtship mode," I said teasingly, "that is not the reason for me refusing your assistance. In truth, the pitiful state of your fridge and pantry gives me hope it means you don't like cooking much."

"Really?" she asked, looking at me as if I'd grown a second head.

"Mmhmm," I said, nodding my head while putting the potatoes to boil. "I love cooking. I claim the kitchen as my domain and would rather not have to chase you out for trying to usurp my place."

She burst out laughing, the lovely sound washing down over me like a gentle caress.

"Well, Mr. Gorgeous Lyrian, the kitchen is all yours," Kathleen said as if I'd agreed to do all her chores for free—which I semi-did. "I don't hate cooking, but I don't particularly love it either. In truth, I'm a huge slacker when it comes to cooking, especially when it's only for myself. You have no idea about the embarrassing amount of food I end up trashing because I let it spoil in the fridge. So, now I try to buy only the strict minimum to avoid wasting so much."

"Rejoice then," I said with a grin. "Your wasteful days are over. You now have a home chef who literally knows over a million recipes from both Earth and the countless planets of Alpha Centauri. Unless you specifically request a repeat of a dish, you will never eat the same thing twice. Even with three meals a day, every day, it would take over nine hundred years for us to taste every recipe I know."

"You can add a couple of snacks a day and maybe a four or five course meal on the weekends?" Kathleen shamelessly offered.

It was my turn to burst out laughing. "That can totally be

arranged," I said with a nod. "And we'll still need over three hundred years without tasting everything."

"Yep, you are definitely a keeper," she said, smiling as I gave a piece of lettuce to Worf who was intently staring at me preparing the food.

He snagged it from my hand with a huge gummy grin, before his sharp teeth began protruding. The Fudian sat down on the counter at a reasonable distance from the food preparation area, his bulging belly almost hiding his short legs before he started to greedily munch on the leaf. He was beyond adorable. Although more primitive, his emotions were also very lovely, pure, and innocent. Despite his initial shyness, the way he'd quickly opened his heart to me touched me deeply. I didn't know his story, but he clearly wasn't one to easily give his affection, which made the gift all the more precious.

Kathleen caressed Worf's own little crown, oddly similar to mine, which made him hoot before resuming his snack. My mate was so perfect. Being with her was natural and effortless. I didn't feel the need to check what I said or did like at the Hive. I was considered too blunt, too impulsive, too emotionally driven. How could I not be? I was an Empath. Of course, I reacted to emotional triggers.

Normally, I shouldn't have played with Worf the way I had in her absence and without her express consent. Pet owners could be very possessive and controlling as far as other people inter-acting with their baby. But my Kathleen had not minded, quite the opposite. Even cuddling her in my arms after that massage was normally a no-no, especially in our situation since she hadn't fully accepted me as a partner yet. Physical interactions with our new partner should only be initiated after an official verbal consent on their part. But it had been the right thing to do. My instincts had said as much, and my woman's response had confirmed its accuracy.

She was made for me and I for her.

I seized the opportunity to thoroughly question her about her food preferences, allergies, dislikes, eating schedules, etc. While I was putting the final touches to the dishes, Kathleen set the table. It wasn't the fancy first meal I had hoped to prepare for my mate to impress her, but I was pleased with the taste and presentation.

"By the way, how do you know so much stuff?" Kathleen asked while taking out the dishes and utensils to set the table. "How does anyone learn so many languages, recipes, types of massages, combat techniques, and all that in a single lifetime?"

Although she had said this nonchalantly, I sensed her underlying unease. I instinctively guessed at the thoughts troubling her. I tilted my head to the side and smiled.

"I'm not a cyborg, if that's what you're thinking," I said teasingly. "And I don't have some sort of memory chip stuck in my brain."

She scrunched her face with that embarrassed expression I was starting to grow familiar with. It was either that or chewing her bottom lip—both of which were adorable.

"We learn in that state of semi-stasis we enter right at the start of puberty," I explained. "Unlike humans, a Lyrian's reproductive organs do not become functional before seventeen—at the earliest. It is also when our empathic abilities go from basic to fully developed. Most of us are between eighteen and twenty before it happens. By then, we have clear tastes and preferences which guide the things we want to learn."

I brought the bowl containing the mixed mashed potatoes and the crab cakes to the table, then went back to get the salad and the dressing on the side. Kathleen poured us a glass of iced tea while Worf jumped down the counter to climb his way on top of the table.

"During that period," I continued, "our brains are like infinite sponges that absorb absolutely everything thrown their way. Since we're in semi-stasis, we don't get bored or restless. But that ends the day we bond," I said, gesturing for her to take a seat before starting to serve some food on her plate. "Once that happens, we start learning the same slow way everyone else does. And this is why I'm asking you so many questions. I want to be able to absorb as much knowledge relevant to you as possible before we bond."

"I presume if *I* had applied instead of my sister, you would have already gotten all of that information," she said.

"Exactly," I replied with a smile.

She eyed her plate with delight. "This looks and smells absolutely delicious," she said with enthusiasm. "Bon Appetit!"

I held my breath while Kathleen took her first bite. Although I knew my food to be good, I'd never cooked for a human before. And this human mattered more than any other.

Her moan as she chewed her first bite of the crab cakes lifted a weight off my shoulders while filling me with pride.

"It's soooo good!" she exclaimed as soon as she swallowed. "How the hell did you pull that off? If I hadn't seen you making this, I'd believe you had it delivered!"

She took a bite of the mashed potatoes and moaned again.

"Imagine what I'll be able to make once I have a proper selection of fresh produce and a full pantry," I said with a silly grin on my face.

"You're totally getting everything and anything you need to keep cooking like this," she said greedily, before giving Worf a piece of crab cake and then pouring some of my vinaigrette on her salad.

Kathleen all but inhaled her food before taking seconds. I couldn't stop smiling. My human taste buds—surprisingly sensitive—were also enjoying the meal. But my woman's emotion enhanced the whole experience.

Halfway through her second helping, Kathleen gave me a strange look.

"What?" I asked.

"I'm wondering what you are right now," she said sheepishly. "Are you Lyrian? Human? A mix of both?"

"I am fully Lyrian right now and will remain as such until we are bonded," I answered. "I'm merely shifted into a human. In that form, our body uses the same function as the species we're emulating."

"So… You could shift to your normal form?" Kathleen asked with a spark in her eyes that spelled trouble.

I barely kept myself from squirming on my chair. "Technically speaking, yes, I could," I conceded. "However, we never do that."

"Why not?" she asked with a slight frown. "Is it forbidden?"

This time, I shifted in my seat. "Well, it's not specifically spelled out in our rules, but it just never happens," I replied. In truth, I'd likely get in trouble if Jarak heard of me doing it. Then again, when did I ever follow rules? "Clean your plate, and I'll show you," I said teasingly.

Instead of complaining, as I had expected, Kathleen literally gulped down the contents of her plate before flat out licking it.

"There, all cleaned," she said, plopping her plate back down a little more forcefully than necessary.

I stared at her, mouth gaping, before bursting out laughing. Worf hooted in response. He had no idea what was funny, but our cheerful mood was contagious.

"Alrighty then," I said, rising to my feet.

I immediately started feeling self-conscious. Few humans had extensively interacted with aliens, many of them having never even met one in the flesh. What if my appearance turned her off or frightened her? I swallowed hard before shifting back to my natural form.

Until now, I'd never really paid attention to my metamorphosis. But this time, I watched to see what she saw. My skin looked like it was melting, its color darkening to become like liquid silver. My limbs narrowed while my body stretched, making my height almost a second full head above her. Thankfully, my skin-tight shorts continued to hug my body, despite it being more slender.

To my relief, awe and extreme curiosity emanated from Kathleen as she studied me. Undaunted, Worf ran on top of the table and stopped next to me to touch my skin. I moved my arm closer to him so that he wouldn't need to stretch so much. Fudians were famous for landing gracefully onto their feet even from great heights. But with his stunted legs, I didn't know how he would fare.

Kathleen approaching me reclaimed my full attention. She raised a hand to touch me then hesitated, her head lifting up to look at me inquisitively. I nodded with a smile. I didn't know how much she could read the expression on my face seeing how indistinct Lyrian features were. A violent shiver coursed through me when the warmth of her palm settled on the bare skin of my shoulder.

I'd never been touched in my normal form by a non-Lyrian hand. And even those contacts had been very scarce once we had been old enough to care for our own basic needs. Like everything else in my world, it had aimed at reducing the risk of us developing certain habits that could hinder our future relationship with our partner. At the time, it hadn't bothered me. But now that I had felt the bliss of cuddling, I couldn't imagine going back to a life where tender physical contacts were frowned upon.

"Don't stop," I whispered when Kathleen hesitated again. "It's as much a new experience for me as it is for you."

More shivers ran through me as her hand slowly roamed over me. I wished I wasn't wearing that damn shirt for greater contact. Her fingers then began exploring my nearly non-existent features, lingering for a moment on my crown. It was a good thing I was currently in my Lyrian form. Had I been human, my erection would be rearing its head again with a vengeance. As she hadn't seen the end of the video, since my awakening had interrupted her, Kathleen hadn't heard Jarak say that our crown was highly erogenous. Touching it signaled to a Lyrian that she wanted to have sex. Her fingers tracing the bony ridges of my crown might as well have been stroking my cock. Thankfully, Lyrians had full control over their bodies, and my phallus didn't extrude despite its burning envy to do so.

I bowed my head to give her greater access to my horns. It tickled when she fiddled with them, making me chuckle. However, a sudden wetness clasping down on my tail startled me. I straightened abruptly, ripping my horns out of Kathleen's grasp and yelped. She also yelped, taking a frightened step back while I looked over my shoulder at what was happening to my tail. Worf, staring at me with his huge black eyes, the two-pronged tip of my tail engulfed in his mouth, appeared to be waiting for me to toss him.

"Seriously?" I whispered before wagging my tail and flicking it towards the living room.

Worf did a couple of aerial flips before landing gracefully on his feet and hooting with pleasure.

"You have a tail!" Kathleen exclaimed.

"I do," I said, matter-of-factly. She gave me the strangest look and then suddenly emitted some strong waves of guilt and self-recrimination. "What? What shameful thought crossed your mind just now?"

She once again scrunched her face in that 'guilty-as-charged' way I'd expected. "Nothing."

"Kathleen," I said in a warning tone.

She made a face at me like I was being utterly unreasonable and then hugged her midsection. "I'm a Xenobiologist. I can't help the thoughts that cross my mind."

My jaw dropped as understanding dawned on me. "You want to dissect me?!"

"NO!! Not at all!" she exclaimed, sincerely horrified—thank the Gods. "I'm not the slasher type."

"But you're a needle-stabber and a sample collecting fiend," I countered.

"At least I don't hurt my subjects," she said with an unrepentant shrug. "And it was just a thought, not an actual plan or intention. It's your fault for being fascinating. Do you hate me now?"

Although Kathleen had said it in a playful fashion, I could feel the uncertainty emanating from her. I shifted back to my human form and drew her into my embrace. To my utter delight, she came willingly.

"Here's your answer," I said before starting to sing. "Nothing's gonna change my love for you. You oughta know by now how much I love you…"

"Oh my God!" Kathleen exclaimed, falling into step as I started to slow dance with her. "That's one of my favorite oldies."

I'd figured as much as she had sung it in the 'Kathleen Bad Karaoke" video Clarisse had sent us.

She tightened her hold around me and buried her face in my neck while I continued singing. In a blur of green scales, Worf ran at dizzying speed, jumping on top of the table in one big leap, before bouncing onto my shoulder. He settled in the crook of my neck opposite from Kathleen and uttered a small hoot. My arms tightened around my woman, and I gently rubbed my cheek on top of the head of the little Fudian. In that instant, I knew beyond any doubt that I had found my family.

CHAPTER 8
KATHLEEN

I reluctantly let go of Anders when he stopped singing. If nothing else, his own reluctance made me feel better. Seeing Worf still hugging Anders's neck did weird things to me. Sure, a little pang of jealousy manifested itself, but happiness superseded it. It gave me a clear green light to continue exploring my growing attraction to the Lyrian. Who would have thought the perfect man could come through home delivery?

I shamelessly enjoyed the view as he leaned over the table to pick up the dishes. The care he took doing so to avoid Worf falling only made me melt further for him.

"So, you can take any appearance you wish?" I asked as I joined in to help him clean the table.

"Pretty much anything, within reason," Anders said with a nod. "But there are size limitations. I could grow to be slightly taller than my default Lyrian form, and much broader. But the muscle mass would look atrophied at the time of bonding. I would need to eat and train to fill up that bigger mass over time."

Although he replied factually, something in the way he said it drew my attention.

"Did my question bother you?" I asked.

"No," Anders said.

"But?" I insisted.

He hesitated before putting the dishes in the sink. Worf ran down his arm to settle at the edge of the sink. "I have this persistent, nagging feeling that you are not quite pleased with my appearance. Do you want me to change my body or my face?"

"No," I said with conviction. "Like I said previously, you're gorgeous."

"Yes, you have said that, and I can sense that you mean it," Anders replied. "However, if *you* had personally requested a Lyrian instead of having one gifted to you, is this the appearance you would have wanted for your partner?"

It was my turn to hesitate, and Anders's shoulders immediately slumped. That broke my heart. Initially, the temptation to lie almost made me say that I would have probably chosen that look, if only to appease him. However, I clearly remembered the video's guidelines instructing me not to lie to a Lyrian, especially during the bonding phase. It would fuck with his empathic bond to me as my words would contradict what he was perceiving from me.

"Look, I honestly love your appearance," I said at last. "If *I* had applied for a mate, I would have chosen a very tall black man with muscles for days and the type of deep voice that makes the floor vibrate beneath your feet. My father is a big black man, and that has shaped my view on what my ideal husband would look like."

Anders's shoulders slumped even more. Despite my lack of empathic abilities, I could feel his disappointment.

"I am sorry for so badly missing the mark," he said in an apologetic voice. "Thankfully, we're not bound. I will make new models until I create one that perfectly meets your expectations."

"That is absolutely out of the question," I said in a tone that brooked no argument.

Anders recoiled, and a sliver of fear crossed his beautiful blue eyes. "What do you mean? You do not want me?"

I closed the distance between us, discarded the sponge in his hand with which he'd been cleaning the dishes to put them in the dishwasher, and took both of his hands in mine. His breathing picked up, becoming slightly shallow with worry while his eyes flicked between mine.

"So far, I love everything about you, Anders, and that includes your appearance," I said in all sincerity. "I may have been a little hesitant when you were delivered in front of my doorstep, but I've never had such a wonderful blind date—or date, period—with anyone before you. I definitely want to get to know more about you and see where it will take us."

With each of my words, tension bled out of Anders only to be replaced by confusion.

"Then why won't you let me take on the appearance of your dream man?" he asked.

"Because, if I had never met you before, then sure, I would have been fine with designing your appearance to whatever my fancy might have been," I explained softly. "But I have met Anders, and he looks like Sean Novak's little brother. This is who you are to me, and this is who is currently sweeping me off my feet."

"But—"

"Do you want me to change my appearance?" I interrupted.

"What?" Anders asked, taken aback.

"You didn't get to choose my appearance. Your Screener said our personalities were highly compatible, and the videos my sister sent you convinced you that might indeed be the case. But you didn't get to choose my appearance," I said. "I'm not a slob, but I'm not the primping doll type of girl either. Do you wish you could change that side of me?"

"Your appearance is irrelevant to a Lyrian," he countered, as if that was self-evident. "Only your personality, as conveyed through your aura, matters to me. For what it's worth, I find you beautiful physically, too. The beauty of your aura only makes you even more stunning to me."

"Exactly," I said, gently. "I may not perceive auras, but who you've shown yourself to be so far is amazing. It only makes your gorgeous appearance even more stunning. For humans, true love is falling for someone else, just the way they are. I do not want to shape you into what I think is the perfect man. I simply want to fall in love with who you are and with all the wonderful ways we can make each other feel."

Anders smiled, his face melting into something akin to adoration that totally messed me up. "I knew you were worth the risk," he whispered.

My brain never registered his face approaching, until his lips pressed against mine. Too stunned to react at first, I didn't resist when he carefully freed his hand from mine and drew me into his embrace. I gripped the see-through fabric of his shirt and melted against him as his lips parted to demand entry.

Holy mackerel, that dude was a good kisser! It was all the crazier knowing that I was the first woman he'd ever kissed—I was his first everything. A firebolt exploded in the pit of my stomach as he tilted his head to the side to deepen the kiss. If he'd become this skilled a kisser through his stasis training, what other naughty things had he mastered?

I was about to tear his shirt off when he broke the kiss, leaving me feeling bereft… and utterly cheated. I whimpered in disappointment, which made him chuckle.

"I shouldn't have done that without your express permission," he said with a voice gravelly with desire. "But I will not apologize for it."

"You had better not," I mumbled.

He chuckled again, brushed my lips with his, then straightened before releasing me.

"According to your sister, this would now be your TV-watching time," Anders said. "Why don't you go pick something for us while I finish cleaning up?"

"You know, you really should let me help with the chores," I argued, feeling like the lousiest hostess in the history of mankind.

He gave me a look that made me swallow any further argument I might have thought of. Tucking my virtual tail between my legs, I skedaddled out of my own kitchen—or should I say Anders's new kitchen—and sauntered over to the living room. I no sooner plopped myself on the couch than Worf came running to me. He jumped on my lap and headbutted Mr. Pudge.

"Boop!" he exclaimed before lying down on his back in my lap.

I giggled and started poking his round belly with my index finger, saying 'boop' each time. Worf hooted, and his short legs wiggled.

"What are you doing to poor Worf?" Anders asked, amused.

"I'm booping him!" I said, matter-of-factly, as if it was a well-known game, before laughing. "Boop is pretty much the only word he can pronounce aside from his hooting sound. So, he uses it for everything. But whenever you actually speak of a 'boop' it means bumping someone's belly with the forehead or poking it with a finger."

Anders blinked, unsure how to respond, which only made me laugh more. It was completely silly, but it had become a custom between my little Fudian and me.

"Oookay. So, when am I getting booped?" he asked.

"Oh no, not you," I replied with a commiserating look. "You need to have a bulging belly for that."

"You don't have a bulging belly, and he booped you," Anders argued.

I snorted. "You haven't seen me naked."

"I've seen Mr. Pudge," he countered. "And I hardly call that a bulging belly. I believe humans call it love handles. That's a lovely name."

My jaw dropped, and then heat crept up my cheeks. "Clarisse included that part in the video she sent you guys?" I exclaimed.

"Yes," Anders said with a nod. "She sent the entire call."

"Oh God!" I said, hiding my face in my hand.

"Why are you embarrassed?" Anders asked, sounding genuinely surprised. "That and you trying to shake Worf off your toe are the first things that seduced me about you. It was so adorable."

"Right," I said, still feeling a little mortified.

I picked up Worf, rubbed my face on his belly then booped him one last time with my forehead before sitting him on my shoulder. He curled up against my neck and started fiddling with my hair.

"Anything you'd like to watch?" I asked while turning on the TV.

"I don't know human movies or television shows. Surprise me," he said, while wiping down the counter before heading my way.

I chewed my bottom lip while debating what to watch. Normally, I would put on a futuristic series. Most of them were struggling to remain relevant as technology kept catching up to them at mind-boggling speed. I also enjoyed the far too rare fantasy movies and series. When nothing new was available, I would usually fall back on some remastered Old Earth classics. There was something oddly enjoyable about their horrendous special effects that had probably been cutting-edge technology at the time.

As I browsed through the guide, I stumbled on a contemporary young adult romance that was trending right now. I hadn't seen it yet. Just from the synopsis, I could tell it would be cheesy, but I occasionally liked my sappy romance. But wouldn't that bore Anders? At the same time, wasn't the point of the first couple of weeks for him to assess our compatibility by having him experience a mix of all the things I was into?

I scrunched my face—a bad habit Mom had told me a billion times to get under control—and glanced at Anders.

"Prepare to be subjected to every boyfriend's worst nightmare; the chick flick," I said sheepishly. "If you really hate it, let me know, and I'll switch to something else."

Anders chuckled. "The whole point is for you to show me the things you are into to determine how compatible we are," he said, echoing the thoughts that had just crossed my mind. "Anyway, if you enjoy it, there's no way I'll hate it. Your pleasure will become mine."

He settled on the couch next to me then, to my utter surprise, drew me in his lap. Worf moved onto his shoulder, and I relaxed against Anders. I had often wished for a movie night at home, cuddling with a special someone. I couldn't believe it was happening now and with someone so perfect... too perfect?

I launched the movie. As it started playing, Anders gently kissed my cheek then wrapped his arms around my stomach. I immediately stiffened, startling him. He looked at me questioningly, and I chewed my bottom lip while trying to hold in my stomach. Yeah, he had seen Mr. Pudge on a video, but to have him touching my belly fat suddenly made me super self-conscious. Sitting down made it worse because it all bunched up like a fanny pack. Moving his hands up would only draw his attention even more to it, and I didn't see myself holding my gut in the entire duration of the movie.

"You became very agitated and uneasy the minute I wrapped my arms around you," Anders said in confusion. "Or more precisely, the moment my hands touched your stomach. I perceive no pain from you, only embarrassment. Why?"

I squirmed, trying to think of an appropriate response, while knowing I couldn't bullshit him with that damn empathic ability of his.

"You do not like me touching your stomach?" he insisted.

"It's… Ugh… Okay, here it goes," I said, feeling mortified and annoyed with myself for feeling that way.

I'd been so proud of my body confidence for years, I hadn't expected to fall back into that sense of insecurity the minute I finally started dating again.

"Humans have this image of the perfect body versus a healthy body. We've come a long way from the crazy period where society expected women to be bags of bones to be considered sexy," I said, proud that my voice didn't shake. "But it's still a thing to want to be sexy for our significant other. I've never been a skinny girl, nor will I ever be. I've always been okay with that. And yet, right now…"

"Right now, you're fearing that I will be less attracted to you because of Mr. Pudge," Anders concluded for me when my voice trailed off. "If I didn't feel your distress, I would be upset that you would think me so shallow. I cannot relate to that human perspective. Like I said, Lyrians do not care about appearances. Your aura is all that matters. As for Mr. Pudge," he said, grabbing my belly with both hands and giving it a squeeze, "he was part of the package that was flaunted before me to lure me here. You do not get to deny me from playing with him now."

I snorted, unable to decide if I wanted to die of embarrassment, laugh, or hug him for being so awesome.

"When you boop Worf or rub his belly, all I perceive from you is how adorable you find its roundness," Anders said. I nodded as I indeed thought it was the loveliest thing in the world. "When Worf boops you, how do you think he thinks of your stomach?"

My face heated at the same time as my heart melted. "He loves Mr. Pudge and often treats him like a pillow. He loves hugging it."

"Why would it be any different for me?" Anders asked gently. "He loves Mr. Pudge because he loves you. You aren't self-conscious when he touches it. You have no reason to ever be self-conscious about me touching you in any way. I like everything about you, just the way you are. So, no more silliness. Understood?"

I nodded, my throat too constricted to speak.

"Good," he said, before kissing my forehead. "Now, you should probably rewind that movie because you made me miss the beginning, you evil woman."

I laughed and playfully elbowed him while rewinding. I stopped then turned to look at him. "You're *really* growing on me, Mr. Anders," I said before kissing his cheek.

"Excellent. My plan of conquest is working," he said shamelessly, his arms tightening gently around me.

More content than I'd felt in years, if not ever, I cuddled against my… boyfriend? We watched the cliché romantic comedy between a geeky girl and a jock embarrassed to let the world know that he was falling hard for her. Although I could see every twist and turn coming a mile away, I still got teary eyed or laughed right on cue. While Anders appeared to enjoy the movie, he was seriously annoyed with the jock. That made me like him even more.

By the time we called it a night, I couldn't help kicking myself for having sent him to the guest room. At the same time, one look at my spinster nightwear collection had me seriously cringing. Between them and my granny panties, I wouldn't win any seduction contests.

I donned a pajama shirt and went to bed.

CHAPTER 9
KATHLEEN

As expected, the tossing and turning game began as soon as I laid my head down on the pillow. Tonight, it promised to be epic. When I wasn't wondering what he was up to, I was berating my sister for not including some sexy lingerie with the comfy clothes she had sent me. You couldn't send someone like Anders to me and not account for the fact that my wardrobe looked like hand me downs from our grandmother. Then again, knowing Clarisse, she'd certainly done it on purpose to shame me into making at least some efforts to be a bit more fashionable.

Despite the excellent soundproofing, the shuffling noises from the guest room, muffled though they were, hinted at Anders cleaning the mess I'd asked him to sleep in. I felt mortified just thinking about it. I should have given him my bedroom and used the guest room instead until I had it properly sorted out. In the minutes that followed, rather than trying to fall asleep, I found myself trying to figure out what specifically he was interacting with, based on the sound.

Giving up, I sat at the edge of my bed and looked for an excuse to go play peeping tom. Worf often—but not always— slept in my bed, either cradling my neck or balled up at my feet.

With his endless curiosity, he was likely 'bothering' poor Anders. It was therefore my duty, as the good hostess that I was still failing to be, to go make sure Worf didn't disturb his sleep.

I made my way to his room then pressed my ear against the door to listen in, more confused than ever. The discreet hum of the vacuum mixed with the shuffling sounds of boxes moving, but I could also hear water in the background. I knocked. No response. I knocked again, but still nothing. I carefully opened the door to peek in, figuring the noise was drowning out my knocking.

My heart skipped a beat, and my blood turned to ice at the sight of a massive dark blob, with close to a dozen tentacles. Four of them were lifting a couple of boxes, while a fifth was vacuuming underneath them. Two more tentacles, each holding a cloth, were wiping down the dusty surfaces. And my little Worf was dangling at the end of an eighth tentacle.

I screamed and jumped a step back. In my fright, I'd shoved the door away from me. It slammed against the wall with a loud clang. Worf yelped, letting go of the tentacle, and placed his back against the wall. His body swelled, ready to go into combat mode to protect me. Startled, the creature spun around. It looked like someone had split its skull open, leaving the brain exposed. Its massive, telescopic eyes could almost have belonged to a chameleon. It didn't possess a visible nose, but the mouth looked like two very short elephant trunks filled with teeth. I screamed again and plastered myself against the door while my heart frantically tried to beat its way out of my chest.

The creature dropped everything it was holding, the ruckus failing to drown out the humming of the vacuum. One of the boxes fell on one of the tentacles of the creature. It hissed with the most obnoxious nail on glass sound before yanking its tentacle free. I watched in morbid fascination as it appeared to melt like so much wax before taking on the liquid silver color I had seen before. The creature gradually shifted back to Anders's human appearance.

"Calm down, Kathleen. It's me, Anders," he said in a soothing voice, his palms raised in an appeasing gesture. "Everything is fine."

My brain had known, but the rest of me didn't give a fuck about logic. There had been a tentacle blob monster in my guest room. Freaking out was the natural response under such circumstances. Running out would have been even smarter, but my brain had vetoed that course of action. Even my poor Worf seemed utterly confused as he started to deflate back to his normal size, having never found the source of my terror.

"Wh… what the heck was that?" I asked, my breathing still a little too fast.

"An Eralgee," Anders said carefully.

He glanced at the bed and slowly walked towards it. I eyed him warily, feeling guilty at his slight wince as he walked. That box must have squished his foot. I then realized he was reaching for his shorts as he was once more buck naked. It made sense as his clothes would have never worked on that blob monster's form.

"They have the perfect body to multi-task," he added apologetically. "If I had known you were going to drop by, I would have warned you. Was I making too much noise?"

I shook my head, still trying to regain my composure. However, that didn't stop me from enjoying the scrumptious sight of his perfectly round behind while he put his shorts back on.

Normally, strange creatures didn't freak me out. After all, as a Xenobiologist, studying strange lifeforms was my thing. But they usually didn't make a random appearance in my guest room to tidy shit up.

"That's a real species?" I asked, my voice slightly shaky.

"Yes. They are one of the most advanced species in Alpha

Centauri. More than a third of all pairings with Lyrians are with them."

"You *marry* that species?!" I exclaimed, feeling immediately embarrassed for the uncharitable reaction.

Thankfully, instead of being offended, Anders looked amused. "Yes. In truth, I always thought I'd become an Eralgee once I mated. Tentacles are quite practical."

"And their voice is incredibly sexy," I said, shuddering again while remembering the horribly grating sound he had made.

Anders burst out laughing. "Right, that takes some major getting used to for strangers. But to an Eralgee, it is very sweet and soothing."

"I bet," I mumbled. "You know, I've never considered myself as superficial, but I couldn't be sexually attracted to you if that had been your natural and permanent form. It shames me to admit it—"

"Don't be," Anders said, becoming serious again. "Your entire life, you've learned a certain definition of beauty for a compatible mate. Humans, like many other Earth species, have physical traits and attributes that help entice a potential partner, like colorful feathers or scales, mating songs, or dances. It is normal that appearance plays a part at least in your initial attraction to someone. With time, and getting to know me, I believe I could have seduced you, even with an Eralgee body. However, as you would never understand my speech, and my voice would destroy your eardrums, I concur that you mating with that species will never happen."

I made a face at him, relieved that he took it so well. "Thanks for making me feel better about being superficial."

He laughed again. "Don't be so hard on yourself," he said kindly while picking up the mess he had made when I'd startled him.

I gave him a hand, impressed by all that he had accomplished in such a short time.

"By the way," Anders said, a sheepish look descending on his handsome face, "when Jarak contacts you for my evaluation, I would be grateful if you didn't mention this little incident."

I stopped to look at him. "Why?" I asked suspiciously. "Did someone do something they weren't supposed to?" I added teasingly.

Anders made a face and squirmed. "Yeah. I'm definitely *not* supposed to do that. Showing you my true form earlier was questionable, but not officially against the rules. My people normally never leave Lyria without being bonded. So, their ability to shift back to their normal form is gone. However, using another species' form to give us an unfair advantage, be it for chores or anything else, is an absolute no-no."

"Why do I have a feeling that you got in trouble *all the time* for breaking rules?" I asked, amused.

"Probably because you have great instincts. I drove the Patriarchs insane with my antics," Anders admitted, looking only slightly remorseful.

"Of course, I'd be paired with a rebel," I said teasingly. "We're the coolest kids anyway."

"Agreed," Anders said with a grin. He glanced around the room before turning back to me. "I'm sorry for waking you, but I'm not sorry you're here."

I grinned, feeling a little guilty again. "You didn't wake me. I couldn't sleep. I heard a bit of noise and figured I'd come see if you needed anything, and if Worf was making a pest of himself."

"Everything is fine. In fact, I was just about wrapping up for the night when you arrived," Anders replied.

"Oh okay," I said, suddenly feeling awkward. "Well, I'll let you go to sleep then."

He frowned, looking at me as if I'd just wronged him.

"What?"

"Considering you nearly gave me a stroke and almost crippled me with that box you made me drop by scaring the living daylights out of me, you should cuddle me to sleep," Anders said in the most outrageous, self-righteous, and entitled tone. "I will limp for days, and I'm scared in this strange new place."

I burst out laughing and shook my head in disbelief at him. "You are absolutely shameless!"

He gave me a sharp nod. "Yes. I've been told that many times."

Still chuckling, I glanced at his foot. "Should I have a look at it for you?"

"No. It will heal overnight if you let me spoon you," Anders said.

"How do you know what spooning is?" I asked, placing my fists on my hips and giving him a stern look.

"On my way here from Alpha Centauri, I've learned every single term, customs, and courtship rituals from Earth," Anders said proudly. "That said, I am focusing on the North American traditions since you humans are all over the place. And even then, they tend to contradict each other."

I laughed again. "We are a mess, but that's what makes us so special."

"So it seems," Anders said with a smile.

He went to close the bedroom door, then slowly walked back to me. My stomach fluttered when he extended a hand towards me. Despite feeling a little shy, I took his hand without hesitation. The way he smiled at me, with so much tenderness and gratitude in his eyes, turned me into a puddle.

Anders led me to the bed. To my surprise, he lay down first, before yanking me towards him. I yelped as I landed on top of him, and then burst out laughing.

"You silly man, you scared me!" I exclaimed, giving him a playful tap on the shoulder.

"Sorry," Anders replied, his voice devoid of the slightest sliver of remorse.

He rolled us to the side and held me snugly, my back pressed to his chest. He nuzzled my nape while pulling the cover over us. Worf hopped onto the bed and hooted a couple of times. His little face flicked between Anders and me with a confused expression. I gestured with my hand for him to approach. He waddled with his duck-like gait on his short legs, which made his round belly sway from side to side.

To my surprise, he climbed on top of me to go boop Anders's forehead, then climbed right back in front of me to boop mine as well, before cuddling against my chest.

"You see, even Worf recognizes I need some TLC for my booboo," Anders whispered in my ear.

"You really have no shame," I whispered. "Lights off!" I called out, plunging the room in darkness. Then I snuggled with a purr against my alien.

CHAPTER 10
ANDERS

I slowly emerged from my natural slumber. After so many years in semi-stasis, it felt both odd and wonderful, especially because of the beauty in my arms. Sleep had never been so amazing, surrounded and infused by the gorgeous aura of my mate. My eyelids fluttered open, surprised at first by the dim light inside the room. I realized then that the large TV screen seamlessly embedded in the wall, displayed a fake window with the shades drawn, but with light seeping in from the sides.

The clever technology acted as a daylight lamp to simulate natural sunlight. A number of bases built in environments hostile to settlers used similar systems to reduce the negative effects of living in a form of confinement. As a Lyrian, my glowing eyes allowed me to see clearly even in a pitch-black environment. But in my current human form, I would have been blind without this fake daylight.

I seized the opportunity to admire my woman. Kathleen moved *a lot* in her sleep. She also muttered unintelligible gibberish between two snores. Right now, she had partially climbed on top of me, with one leg over mine, her arm around my chest, and her head on my shoulder. Her shirt had ridden up exposing her round behind and the white panties that contrasted beautifully with her brown skin. Her face was puffy with sleep, and her cheek bore the mark of her pajama shirt's fabric when she'd rested her head on her arm. The steady sound of her snoring reminded me of a purring cat. And her curly hair, so soft and fragrant, looked like a tornado had rampaged through it.

My Kathleen was so fucking adorable!

I wanted to squeeze her in my arms and cover her face with kisses. But that would wake her. Although subdued in her sleep, Kathleen's emotions indicated both happiness and the need for further rest. However, it would soon be time for her to go to work. With much reluctance, I carefully extricated myself from my woman and got out of bed. Worf had curled up in a ball at the foot of the bed during the night. It had no doubt been to avoid getting squished with all of Kathleen's tossing and turning. He perked up and made a discreet hoot, not to wake her.

Although limited, the intelligence of the little Fudian impressed me. But above all, his unconditional love for my mate moved me. And what a big heart in such a little body. I didn't doubt for a second that Worf would gladly give his life to protect Kathleen if needed. That he had so openly welcomed me into their inner circle touched me beyond words. I extended a hand towards Worf. He jumped on top of it then climbed his way to my shoulder before hugging my neck. The little rascal, too, was stealing a piece of my heart.

Careful not to wake Kathleen, I exited the bedroom and closed the door behind me. After settling Worf on the counter, I rummaged through the fairly bare fridge to find something to prepare as breakfast for my mate. In one of the cupboards, I found some coffee. Recalling how it apparently was a big thing for humans in the morning, I prepared a fresh pot. I'd just begun making some hash-browns with the remaining potatoes to go with the bacon and eggs when Kathleen stumbled out of the bedroom.

Looking groggy, she rubbed her eyes while crossing the living room. She bumped against the couch and muttered something at it as if the furniture had deliberately gotten in her way. I bit the inside of my cheeks not to laugh.

"Tell me it's coffee I smell," she pleaded.

"It is. Sugar? Milk?" I asked while pouring her a cup.

She frowned and shook her head with a disapproving grunt. I extended the cup to Kathleen who accepted it with both hands. She took a sip, closed her eyes then moaned as if she was on the verge of an orgasm.

"I love you so hard right now," she mumbled before turning on her heels and heading towards her bedroom.

The words struck me like a ball of fire in the gut. Kathleen hadn't meant them *that* way. I just wished she had. I was crazy for her and beyond ready to bond. However, she wasn't. Humans sadly didn't feel auras like we did. My woman's emotions clearly expressed the strong attraction she felt towards me. She was smitten and hopeful for a permanent future between us in the long run, but Kathleen didn't love me. It would be many weeks, likely many, many months before she would truly be in love with me. Now more than ever, I needed to manage my expectations.

I was finishing setting up the table when Kathleen returned from her room, looking refreshed, her wild mane tamed, and properly dressed for work. Although comfortable, her clothes were too big for her. While it didn't bother me, it didn't follow the human fashion codes, and it didn't flatter her beautiful body. I couldn't decide if it was a conversation worth having, and especially worried she might misinterpret my motives for bringing it up. A part of me believed the baggy clothes weren't just a matter of comfort but also a way to hide her perceived flaws.

I refilled her empty cup of coffee, and we sat down to eat.

"Thank you for this. You're truly a godsend," Kathleen said with genuine gratitude. "In the morning, I'm a real grump before I get my coffee and put my human face on."

I chuckled upon hearing the silly expression. "My pleasure."

"I hope I didn't snore too loudly," Kathleen said sheepishly after swallowing another sip of coffee.

"Not at all," I said, amused. "It's the cutest purring sound."

"You're being kind," she said dubiously. "My sister says I sound like an old engine about to keel over. It sputters once every so often, stops, and then revs back up for another agonizing round."

I burst out laughing. Although the imagery was greatly exaggerated, it wasn't entirely false. However, I thought the sounds she made were cute.

"Are human siblings always this brutal with each other?" I asked, before taking a bite of scrambled eggs.

"Oh! That's not brutal at all coming from my sister," Kathleen exclaimed as if I'd said something ludicrous. "That's a love tap at best. Having fun at your sibling's expense is a national sport. You're not a proper sibling if you're not needling them at every opportunity. Didn't you tease your brothers back on Lyria?"

"No, not really," I said, fascinated by this glimpse into human culture. "The family unit on Lyria is quite different than with humans. We have very few females, whom we call Matriarchs. They only represent 15% of our population."

"Oh my God!" Kathleen exclaimed. "That's crazy! No wonder you have to marry alien species."

I nodded. "On average, each Matriarch marries ten Patriarchs. It is a tremendous honor for one of us to be chosen by a Matriarch," I explained. "Naturally, it happens to very few of us. None of my thirty-four siblings were chosen. Therefore, although we know our mother, we do not know which one of her mates is our sire; not that it matters."

"Oh wow," Kathleen said, sympathy laced with sadness for me emanating from her. "I'm sorry."

I chuckled. "For what? Our society is different. A standard

family unit like the humans' would have an undue influence on our perception of what a family should be like. But we do not know what culture we will end up in," I said. "Therefore, it is important for us to have as blank a slate as possible. For what it's worth, it wasn't lonely; not with so many brothers to play with. All of us Fledglings are loved, surrounded by the affection of our Patriarchs and occasionally of our Matriarchs."

"Only occasionally?" she asked.

"Yes. Lyria is a matriarchy. Our mothers are busy running our home world, establishing diplomatic relations with other planets that could be interested in welcoming us as mates, and ironing out the various treaties and agreements with foreign species."

"But isn't it a little complicated raising so many empathic children?" she asked after swallowing a mouthful of her breakfast.

"Not really," I said with a smile. "The Patriarchs raise the offspring of their Matriarch. That's ten males sharing the burden. As Empaths, they fully understand—and often anticipate—the needs of the young. Where human parents try to guess why their child is crying, our Patriarchs feel it and can more easily address it."

"Okay, now *that* is super cool," Kathleen said, impressed. "But, once you mate with someone outside your species, do you lose that ability?"

"No. We remain Empaths forever, regardless of what species we become," I replied smugly. "So, when you and I have children, I'll be able to tell you exactly what you did to cause our brats to throw temper tantrums."

"Wait, what?! Why me?" she exclaimed, falsely outraged. "If anything, Worf will be responsible."

I snorted before nodding. "That will probably also be true."

Kathleen's watch beeped. "Damn it, I have to go to work,"

she said with a frown. "What are you going to do with your time?" she asked, an air of guilt descending on her face.

"I will learn more about the things I found out from you last night, now that I finally have more insight about what you like," I said with a smile.

"Oh good. I'm really a terrible host and a poor planner," she added with an embarrassed expression. "Mom would seriously disown me. I will try to come back and have lunch with you."

"That's not necessary," I said, shaking my head. "I've disrupted your plans enough as it is with my impromptu appearance. And," I added quickly when she opened her mouth to argue, "the learning cycle takes seven hours. I will be in semistasis the whole time."

"All right then," she said, with a sliver of relief. "I'm working on a new splice in parallel with my Kirdie project. Things either go really well and I'm done early. Or they go belly up, and I'll end up pulling an all-nighter. Hopefully, it will be the former."

"You'll nail it," I replied in an encouraging tone. "I have faith in you."

"Thank you," Kathleen said with a grateful smile.

We both got up. To my greatest delight, she approached me and rose on her tiptoes to kiss my cheek. I caught her nape before she could pull away and kissed her lips. She melted against me, instantly lighting a fire in the pit of my stomach. I had only meant for this to be a more intimate kiss goodbye as human couples often did. But this body was insanely responsive. It was a wonder humanity managed to accomplish anything. With how easily they became aroused, you'd think they'd be copulating around the clock. Right now, I just wanted to drag Kathleen back to my bedroom and unleash the repressed passion bubbling inside of me.

I reluctantly released her before my blossoming erection

became too obvious. I didn't want my mate to think me a sex-starved maniac.

"See you later, my beauty," I said while caressing her cheek with my knuckles.

"See you later, Anders," she replied timidly.

Kathleen turned to Worf, who had resumed his usual spot on the table, and leaned down to boop his forehead. He hooted and gave her his version of a toothless grin as she waved us goodbye.

The minute the door closed behind my mate and her intoxicating aura faded out of range, a terrible sense of loss crushed my heart. A part of me wanted to run after her and bring her back here. It was a good thing that she'd had to leave for work. Some short periods of time apart during the bonding phase were essential to prevent empathic addiction. It could lead a Lyrian to lose himself in his mate. Just like with physical training, after an intense session, you needed to let your muscles rest and strengthen before the next round.

Despite that, things were moving in the right direction. Who would have imagined that Anders, the rebel, would find his perfect mate? I cleaned the table and the kitchen, then proceeded to call Jarak for my first day report. It was odd not being able to feel the emotions of my Patriarch. With the Lyrians' barely defined expression, reading what someone was feeling on their faces was nearly impossible. However, I knew beyond any doubt that he was happy for me.

Our next communication would be on day seven, at exactly the halfway point of this 'trial' phase. This insecurity gnawed at me. None of my brothers had ever gone to their Seeker wondering whether she'd keep him or not. Kathleen was falling hard and fast for me, but only twenty-four hours had gone by. How would she feel in one week from now? And worse still, when the second week came rolling in where she would need to commit to bond with me or forever let me go, how would she respond?

The more I learned about humans, the more my situation felt precarious. Their species didn't make lifelong commitments after such a short period of time. They dated for months, even years before taking the final step. Would Kathleen be willing to make such a leap of faith with me? After only twenty-four hours, I was already addicted to her. It was taking every ounce of my willpower not to let the bonding process begin.

If we were to become intimate—and I believed we would soon—should she decide not to keep me, I would be ruined. Truth be told, even if she sent me back tomorrow, it was already too late for me. There was no question in my mind that Kathleen was my soulmate. I could never want another but her.

However, now wasn't the time to be borrowing trouble. I needed to focus my efforts on making sure she, too, could never want another but me. I initiated the download of the top files recommended by the Screener based on the parameters I had entered following my conversations with Kathleen. As it would take a little while for them to be configured on my Mentor device, I seized the opportunity to take a quick shower.

Water showers were an interesting experience, very sensual, unlike the superfast, and highly effective particle showers we used on Lyria. However, humans also possessed that technology. I could therefore only presume water showers were a choice rather than a necessity.

Once done, I picked up the headphone looking device. It emitted a low frequency signal to my brain, which slowed down all of my bodily functions while enhancing my cognitive abilities. Although it could work with a human body, it wouldn't be as effective. I therefore shifted to my Lyrian form before lying down and putting the Mentor on my head.

A holographic display appeared in front of me. Through vocal command, I selected three modules that would total seven hours. The first one focused on nerds, geeks, and misfits in high school and college and its psychological impact on the rest of their lives. Although last night's movie had indeed been trending on the network, I believed Kathleen had subconsciously sought to test my reaction to such a situation. Deep down, she perceived me as the jock. This body indeed matched that description. I was starting to realize that beneath her nonchalant attitude, my mate harbored a great deal of insecurity. For this reason, the other modules covered body shame and self-consciousness, and lack of self-esteem.

"Initiate session," I commanded.

A pleasant heat around my temples was quickly followed by a tingling sensation throughout my body. My eyes closed on their own just as the silhouette of Worf came into my line of sight. I felt him curl up into a ball on my chest just as darkness swallowed me.

❧

The fluffy feel of my woman's mane on my shoulder greeted me as I emerged from partial stasis. It was still extremely odd to feel human skin against my natural form, but I loved that Kathleen felt so comfortable with my true self that she would cuddle with me in this form. However, her emotions were hard to read, almost like when she was sleeping, even though she was currently awake. It was an odd sense of well-being, preoccupation, and something else I couldn't name.

My movement to wrap my arm around her startled my woman. Guilt immediately emanated from her.

"I'm sorry! I didn't mean to interrupt your training!" she said, looking mortified.

I smiled and caressed her hair. "You didn't. My session just ended," I replied in a soft voice. "*I* am the one who is sorry you're already here. I wanted to have dinner ready for you when you walked in."

"Don't be, I came back early," she said. "My new experiment

is currently going through an accelerated form of incubation. So, there's nothing I can do at the moment. But I have to go back in a little less than an hour from now. I doubt I will be back for supper."

Reluctantly letting go of her, I got out of bed to put the Mentor back on its base so that it could recharge for my next session and shifted back to my human form.

"Is there something wrong with the project?" I asked, sensing growing distress from her as she spoke of her work.

She shook her head. "No, not this project. Everything is going beyond smoothly," she said, scooting over to come sit at the edge of the bed.

I sat down next to her and wrapped my arm around her shoulders. She leaned into me, her despair cranking up another notch.

"What is it, my darling?" I insisted, my heart breaking to feel her so distraught.

"Mirik is dying," she said, her voice trembling. "I've done everything I could for him, but he can't make it without his mother's care, and she won't let him near her. I feel like such a failure for not figuring out what's wrong."

"You are not a failure," I said forcefully. "Unfortunately, these things happen. What's wrong with the little one?"

She shrugged. "You don't want to know. It's just depressing stuff."

"If I didn't, I wouldn't have asked," I gently chastised. "I want to know more about you, and what you do. And right now, I feel your pain, and I want to help you shoulder it."

She looked at me with an indefinable expression laced with doubt but also gratitude. Despite her dismissive attitude, Kathleen needed someone to talk to. With her lab partner away for the holidays, she had no one to share her hardships with.

My mate launched into a detailed description of the Kirdie species enhancement project the mining corporation she worked for had tasked her with. Mirik's birth had heralded a resounding success that was now on the verge of becoming an epic failure. She was the lead on the project, and the company had sunk a substantial amount of money towards her research that Kathleen got to spend at her discretion. If she didn't provide results very soon, she would not only be demoted, but the project might be cancelled altogether.

However, it was the death of the little Kirdie that distressed her the most. Kathleen loved hard. And I was beginning to suspect she had a particular soft spot for the misfits and the broken. I wished I had a solution for her, but based on what she shared with me, it indeed sounded like she had done everything humanly possible to save Mirik.

"Thank you for being such a wonderful listener," Kathleen said at last with a tender look in her eyes that made me all fuzzy inside. "I didn't realize how much I needed to unload some of this. You Empaths really are awesome."

"I'm the *only* Empath you need to be impressed with," I mumbled.

She laughed, cupped my face in her hands, and rubbed her nose against mine before kissing my lips. "I think I like you being jealous."

"Good! Because I do not share," I said playfully, and yet seriously.

"Good indeed, because I do not want to be shared."

I smiled and, this time, took the initiative of kissing her. I loved how she immediately responded, her lips parting to welcome my tongue. No other species I knew kissed like that. Most would likely shred each other's mouths and tongues in light of the crazy teeth they possessed. Eralgees especially with their trunk-like mouths filled with teeth would never even contemplate such a thing. And yet, this was incredibly enjoyable. Who would have thought licking the insides of another person's mouth could be this sexually pleasing?

To my chagrin, Kathleen put an end to it just as I was about to become bolder.

"I have to go back," she said, as saddened as I felt. "You probably shouldn't wait up for me."

My heart sank at that prospect, but I put up a brave front. She wouldn't welcome me being clingy. "So long as you promise that you will come cuddle with me when you get home. The monster in the closet is plotting to eat me in my sleep."

She chuckled. "We can't have that now, can we? I will just have to sacrifice myself and come protect you while you dream. In the meantime, I'm sure Worf will keep the meanies at bay."

"Thank you," I said with exaggerated relief.

Kathleen kissed me one last time, quickly 'fixed' her hair in the mirror, and caressed Worf's head before leaving.

"I guess it's just you and me, right, little one?" I said, poking the little Fudian's round belly.

Worf grinned at me with his gums then said, "Boop!"

CHAPTER 11
KATHLEEN

My second experiment was going wonderfully. The first simulations on the enriched protein I'd synthesized to feed Kirdies was looking beyond promising. It wasn't a huge victory, but it would hopefully help pacify my employer in light of the epic failure of my main project.

I was gently rocking little Mirik in my arms, trying to emulate the motion his mother did with his sibling. I also replayed a recording of the sounds she'd make during those times. The poor little one would probably pass in the next twenty-four hours or so. My heart was breaking for him. If only Josie had been back from vacation. Maybe she would have seen something that had escaped me. If not, at least it would have been someone more to talk to.

Anders spared me from being an even bigger mess. He was so amazing in every way, and so incredibly supportive. I'd never dated anyone who'd shown genuine interest in my work. Their eyes would always glaze over. Being with him was effortless. I'd been worried that he might be too focused on 'serving' me to the point it would be an unbalanced relationship with one doing all the giving and the other all the taking.

Thankfully, in the past three days since his arrival—today being the fourth—Anders had seemed open to letting me do things for him as well. On a few occasions, he had clearly expressed his preferences that differed from mine as to what movie to watch, and I had yielded to him. However, he was getting antsy being cooped up inside my living unit. He hadn't brought up the subject yet since he still had quite a bit of stasis learning to do, but it was only a matter of time.

To be honest, I had been burying my head in the sand about it. How was I supposed to introduce him? How would I answer the inevitable questions and snide remarks people would make? The selfish part of me wanted to keep him forever locked up inside my place. Frankly, if I didn't have to go to work, I'd just stay locked inside with him. But that was unrealistic, not to mention that he had already brought up a few potential careers he could take on here on the base. He'd been thinking about jobs that could easily be transplanted to wherever my own career may take me.

In an ideal world, we wouldn't have to address any of these topics for the next ten days until the final decision about us as a couple had to be made. Anders was beyond ready to commit already. And that, too, worried me. He just felt too good to be true. Every day that I went home to him, I held my breath, waiting for the other shoe to drop.

The chime of my com going off startled the living daylights out of me. I glanced at it and groaned inwardly: Patty. I still hadn't gotten back to her about the Christmas party that was only five days away. For sure Anders would want to go. But as much as I dreaded attending parties, this would be a billion times worse with everyone and their brother sticking their noses in my business. That gave me even less time than I thought for me to decide how I wanted to introduce him to everyone. And what if things ended up not working out in the four days that followed before we had to make a final decision?

Fuck me sideways. Why was everything always so complicated?

I carefully placed Mirik back into his smaller vivarium and answered my com. "Hey Patty, sorry I didn't get back to you sooner, things have been a little hectic the past few days," I apologized preemptively.

"Hectic?" she replied, sounding offended. "Talk about the understatement of the year, you sneaky little naughty girl! To think you let me waste my breath trying to hook you up with someone when you knew all along you had something so much better coming your way, you little tramp!"

Although she had said it in a playful manner, the word offended me. But more importantly, her implication had my blood turning to ice in my veins.

"I don't need your answer about the Christmas party anymore," Patty continued, in full gossip mode.

"What do you mean?" I asked in a tensed voice.

"Right this instant, I'm staring at a scrumptious beast of a man named Anders," Patty said, her voice dripping with envy. "How the heck could you afford him? I know what you make, and I've heard what they cost."

"You're in my quarters?!" I exclaimed, both shocked and outraged.

"No, silly. I'm at the grocery store. He's shopping for you, and he isn't much of a talker," she said in a pouty tone. "So? Are the rumors true? Are they insatiably wild in the sack? How hung did you order him? I'm assuming he's your Christmas date, right? Girl, you and I need to talk. Can I come over to your lab?"

"I am *not* discussing Anders with you! He's my personal business. You stay the fuck out of it," I snapped, beyond livid. What the fuck was he doing at the store? "I'll talk to you later."

I hung up, cutting off her shocked voice arguing and stormed out of my lab. As I headed to the grocery store, people I passed in the hallways either cast a wary look my way—no doubt due to my fuming expression—or had a strange smirk that spoke volumes. Within the next hour or so, the news of Anders's presence would spread like wildfire throughout the station. This was *not* how I had wanted the word to get out—if at all.

I could already hear what they would all be thinking. The poor, desperate, Plain Jane of Mars had lost all hope of finding a man who'd want her. So, she'd bought one that had no choice but to love her instead. My cheeks burned with shame as I finally reached the store.

I plastered a neutral expression on my face while every gaze zeroed in on me. Their amused, slightly scandalized, or suggestive expressions upon seeing me enter were mortifying. I wished the protective dome of the station would just open up, suck me right out of the base, and somehow propel me deep into outer space. The reality would be more like passing out from lack of oxygen in seconds followed almost immediately by every single one of my organs rupturing from the lack of atmospheric pressure. But hey, a quick fifteen-second death would beat this humiliation.

To my relief, I didn't have to chase Anders through the aisles as he was already in the process of checking out. Thankfully, he was respectably dressed with long black pants and a nice lightgrey t-shirt, instead of the stripper shorts and see-through top he'd been wearing at home. Moira, the cashier serving him, was ogling him in the least subtle fashion. It was downright disrespectful. Anders's slightly annoyed expression lit up the minute he saw me approaching. But his smile stiffened and somewhat dimmed as he sensed the fury bubbling inside of me.

"Hey Kathleen, lost something?" Moira asked, casting a meaningful glance at Anders, before wiggling her eyebrows in a lurid fashion.

I glared at her. "You're the one about to lose something if you don't keep your fucking eyes to yourself," I snarled. She recoiled, a shocked expression descending on her features. She was a nice enough girl. We'd always been on friendly terms, and she'd never seen me furious, let alone talking this crudely to anyone. "I'm sure the Ethics Committee would seriously frown if they heard about how you've been leering at him."

"Whoa, no need to take it that far," Moira said, blanching. "I meant no disrespect."

"Well, you *were*," I snapped back. "When you're done ringing this stuff, please charge it to my account and have it delivered to the cool storage outside my place."

"I was going to pay," Anders argued.

"I got it," I responded sharply in a tone that brooked no argument.

"Certainly, right away," Moira said. "I'm sorry."

"Don't apologize to me. Apologize to *him*."

She mumbled some excuses at Anders. He nodded and distractedly gave her a stiff smile, before looking at me again with a slight frown.

"Let's go," I said to Anders, marching out before he could answer.

He walked alongside me without speaking a word. The loud sound of my footsteps in the silent hallway made me realize that I was all but stomping my feet. Normally, I would have made a beeline for my quarters, but I needed to go back to the lab. In truth, I shouldn't have walked out while the experiment was still processing in case something went wrong.

Naturally, everyone and their brother decided now was the time to crowd the hallways. Part of me believed someone had spread the word that the Beauty and the Geek—or was it the Sex Bot and the Spinster?—were parading around the base. Therefore, all the gawkers were out to get an eyeful of the freakshow.

After an eternity and a day, we finally reached my lab. I opened the door for Anders and followed him inside. If not for the automatic closing, I probably would have slammed it shut behind me. Anders turned to look at me with an unreadable expression on his face.

I raised my palms questioningly at him and gave him a 'what the fuck' look. "What the hell were you doing at the store?" I asked in a stern voice.

"Wasn't it obvious?" Anders asked, a slight irritation seeping into his voice. "There were a few ingredients missing. I went to acquire them."

"Why didn't you just call me to bring what was missing?" I asked, not in the least pleased by his tone.

"Why would I?" he asked, tilting his head to the side. "You're busy working. I have the spare time and the funds. Waiting for you would also mean delaying the time supper would be served."

"A little delay wouldn't have killed anyone," I ground through my teeth. "I had not given you permission to go lurk around the base."

"Permission?" Anders asked with an expression that clearly expressed he couldn't believe he'd heard me correctly.

This time, anger descended on his beautiful features, and he took one menacing step towards me. Although it intimidated the fuck out of me—and deflated some of my own anger—I didn't fear for my safety. At a visceral level, I knew he would never physically hurt me. But I could sense the impending tongue lashing.

"Am I your prisoner?" Anders asked in a hard voice.

I flinched. "Of course, not. But…"

"But what?" he insisted in that same icy tone that made me want to squirm.

Now that he was putting me on the spot, my initial anger gave way to shame. My mind was working overtime rational-izing my knee-jerk reaction. But I didn't really want to face what it said about me. I shook my head and shrugged.

"In the store and in the hallway, you were humiliated,"

Anders said in a clipped tone. "Every time we passed someone, you avoided making eye contact and got even more mortified. You are ashamed of me, of people knowing that we're together."

"NO! That's not true!" I exclaimed.

"Yes, it is!" Anders snapped. "Have you forgotten that I can read your emotions? You were ashamed to be seen with me. Funny," he added with derision. "On this base, you're the jock and I'm the embarrassing nerd."

That struck me hard. I hugged my midsection and shook my head. It wasn't like that... right? I needed to make him understand...

"It's not like that, Anders," I said in a pleading tone. "You... You are perfect, absolutely gorgeous. But this is my workplace. I have to interact with these people every day. Some of them can be borderline malicious in their teasing. Lyrians aren't common in the Solar System. Whatever status you have in Alpha Centauri, it doesn't exist here. Humans will consider you like a sex toy or a mail order bride."

I nervously ran my fingers through my hair, hating that I couldn't read his emotions right this instant. His handsome face was completely closed off, devoid of any expression. And yet, I could feel him seething within. I also suspected that he was deeply hurt.

"You once asked me if I wanted to make any modifications to your appearance, and I said no," I said carefully. "I meant it at the time. And while I still think you're absolutely perfect, we do not live in a vacuum. It would be a lot easier if you didn't have your crown. It marks you as 'other' and people will only focus on that to spew nonsense. But if you fully looked human—"

"No." My heart sank at the cold finality of his voice. "From a legal standpoint, and in accordance with the galactic treaties, Lyrians are obligated to keep one of their genetic features between the horns, the crown, or the tail. We found the crown suited the human aesthetic best, especially since horns and tails have questionable connotations in some of your religious subcultures."

"Why are you *obligated* to have at least one of those features?" I asked, taken aback.

"Because it is illegal for us to try and pass ourselves off as a species we're not," Anders replied. "Part of the immigration paperwork that is filled out includes a sworn statement that we not do so, unless we get full citizenship on that planet—which requires ten years of residence on most worlds."

"I see," I said, my shoulders slumping.

That seemed to fuel his anger even more.

"And why should I hide what I am?" he snapped. "I am a proud Lyrian. If you mated an alien and moved to his world, how would you feel if he asked you to undergo massive surgery to hide your human genetics?"

I flinched again. That, too, struck a nerve. I'd never really considered it from that angle. He was an alien who had been raised with the idea that he would become a different species once he mated. It had been narrow-minded of me to assume that meant he held no pride about his true origins. In his shoes, I also would have wanted to keep a trace of my ancestry.

"What does it matter if the others think that I'm a sex bot?" Anders asked. "You and I both know it's not true. Most of them also know it—at least deep down—but they simply enjoy being able to bully you. Then they go home to their own partner and enjoy their little lives, while you wallow in self-pity and misery."

"It's not that simple," I feebly argued.

"Yes, it is," Anders snarled. "I can adapt to pretty much anything for my mate. I can change many things about myself to make you happy. But I cannot, and *will not*, change who and what I am to placate a bunch of idiots. *You* must decide if you can live with it. And *that*, Kathleen, is why we've never been 'gifted' to anyone before. We are not sex bots or kinky sex toys that can be hidden away in a drawer or under a mattress in between uses. I will not be your shameful secret."

I was winded. Shame burned in my gut like so much acid. I was searching for the right words to respond, not really knowing what to say, how to soothe the pain I had caused him. It had never been my intention, but my own thoughts were too jumbled to come up with anything coherent.

Anders cast a glance around the room and approached the glass wall separating the antechamber from the lab. He looked at the vivarium where Lily—the Kirdie mother—was surrounded by her four other offspring. She was stealing looks at Mirik, all alone at the other end of the table, in his smaller vivarium.

"As for them, the mother doesn't reject Mirik," Anders said. "She aches for him."

"What? She rejects him every time I bring him to her," I argued, my mind getting whiplash from this sudden change in topic.

"To protect him," Anders replied.

"Protect him from what?" I asked, baffled. "The others?"

"No, they want their brother as well," Anders said.

"Then what?" I asked.

"Why haven't you put some of those varberries in his vivarium?" Anders asked.

I blinked, once more thrown by this switch in topic. "Because he's too young to eat and digest them. Lily used to eat them a lot. It's a treat for Kirdies."

"That is likely your problem," Anders said.

"It can't be," I said, shaking my head. "I tried bringing Lily over to Mirik's vivarium, and even then, she pushed him away."

"Did you wash her first?" Anders asked.

I blinked again, more confused than ever.

"Varberries shed microscopic spores that stick to the fur and scales of the small creatures that feed from them," Anders explained, in a neutral tone. "When those creatures dig holes, they spread the spores to help the plant grow in other areas. The spores are often toxic to Nargun lizards. I do believe that is what you spliced the Kirdie with?"

My jaw dropped as I gaped at him in disbelief. I didn't know for a fact that any of what he had just said was true, but I had no reason to doubt him. Anders was literally a living, breathing encyclopedia.

"How did you figure that?" I asked, winded.

"When I'm not lurking around your base without permission, I spend my time learning everything that could be of relevance to you," he retorted, the sarcasm, hurt, and anger seeping right back into his voice. "I'll go back to my room, now. Unfortunately, I will likely be seen while doing so. I am sorry that I'm not what you wanted."

"Anders…" I called out, not really knowing what to say.

He ignored me and walked out. A part of me wanted to chase after him, but I needed to get my head in order first. Feeling a little numb, I entered the lab, approached the large vivarium, and picked up Lily to give her a bath. Moving on autopilot, I barely even noticed what I was doing, my mind was so overwhelmed.

Each of Anders's words and my own reactions replayed in a loop in my head. He was right. After all these years hating on jocks, I had treated him exactly the same way. It hurt all the more that he had fully accepted me with my endless flaws, and I had only accepted him as long as he remained a secret.

Which meant I hadn't truly accepted him.

Or did I?

As I carefully brought Lily towards Mirik's vivarium, the poor little baby emitted a pitiful whimper with such longing, it tore me up inside. But this time, Lily didn't hiss. She stretched her long, rodent-like head towards his small habitat. My heart leapt with hope. Could it truly have been that simple? I placed Lily inside the vivarium. Tears blurred my vision as the Kirdie, for the first time, rushed over to her baby and immediately began licking him, like she had done with the rest of her offspring. Mirik whimpered and rubbed himself against his mother, weakly clinging to her.

I pulled a chair and sat down in front of the small vivarium, watching mother and son bond, and Lily feeding her baby at long last. Anders had fixed their family. Now, I needed to fix ours.

CHAPTER 12
ANDERS

I had never felt such deep pain. Even on Lyria, when I would get chastised for my constant mischiefs and inability to stick to rules, I'd never felt rejected or unwanted. I was different, and it was okay, even if discipline needed to be meted out to prevent me from disrupting the good order of things. But this…?

In Alpha Centauri, Lyrians were revered. To be mated with one of us was a great source of pride. Too few Seekers received the honor of being chosen by one of my brothers. I understood that this had skewed my expectations as to my experience here. Jarak had warned me that this pairing could be challenging and that the road to our bonding could be difficult if not painful. But I never thought I'd feel so utterly crushed.

The humiliation she had felt anytime someone saw me felt like a rain of acid showering over me. The past few days had been such an illusion in the seclusion of her home.

But she felt horrible when I confronted her.

She had. Shame and remorse had choked Kathleen while we talked in her lab. But once again, we were in private, hidden from view. I didn't know how to handle this situation. Nothing had prepared me for this. Maybe if Lyria had begun advertising our mating program here in the Solar System, the human society would have been better prepared to accept me. Well... accepted wasn't quite the right term. I hadn't felt any rejection on their part, mostly curiosity, confusion, and surprise. They didn't quite know what I was. But above all, they didn't understand why I would be paired with Kathleen.

And *that* was the real issue.

That thought dampened some of my pain but fanned my anger. Whether they believed me to be a sex bot or an alien, they thought me too good for Kathleen, or failed to understand what I saw in her. No wonder she had such low self-esteem, despite her 'I don't care' front.

Kathleen was my soulmate. There were no ifs or buts about it. I could feel it in my bones, all the way through the depths of my soul. Her aura was beyond magical to me. Even now, despite what had just transpired, I longed to bask in her presence again. The Empath in me wanted to bow to her wish and lock myself in her quarters forever. But the individual in me, Anders, refused to bend. I wasn't a dirty little secret. I, too, wanted to be loved and accepted for who I was. While I would greatly adapt to her through the empathic bond, we needed to be equals in this relationship: not mistress-servant.

Heaving a deep sigh, I recovered the groceries delivered to the cool storage locker embedded in the wall next to Kathleen's front door. When I entered the living unit, Worf greeted me with his usual enthusiasm, but he quickly sobered, realizing something was off. I placed the crate with all the food on the counter, then picked up the little green Fudian. I booped his forehead then placed him on my shoulder. The depth of love that emanated from the little creature as he hugged my neck made my eyes prick, while soothing my aching heart.

I gently caressed his back, letting myself be infused with his affection.

"You know, you are something else, little Worf," I said gently.

He lifted his head to look at me with his big, fathomless black eyes, then bumped my cheek with his forehead. "Boop," he said.

"Thank you, my friend," I replied.

He grinned with his toothless smile. Feeling a little better, I put away the groceries and prepared the meal that had triggered this whole mess to begin with. Once done, I fed Worf and placed the food on a warmer. As much as this situation distressed me, I didn't regret it happening. Better address it now than later, when I'd be even more entranced with my woman.

Feeling at a loss as to how to handle the situation, I entered my stasis chamber—which was now standing near the bed—and established a communication with Lyria. Its advanced technology allowed for real-time conversation with minimal delay, despite the great distance.

To my relief, Jarak responded quickly. The signal broadcast his image in my mind's eye and a holographic representation of me to him. Since our next call wasn't due for another three days, the Patriarch immediately knew something had gone wrong. The concerned expression on his face moved me deeply. With our subtle features, the fact that I could so clearly read his emotions merely by looking at him spoke volumes.

"What is wrong, son?" Jarak said in lieu of greeting.

"I feel lost, Patriarch," I said, feeling utterly discouraged. "I love Kathleen with all my heart. I want to wrap myself in her aura and drown in it. She's definitely the one for me. But the human culture and this human body confound me."

"Overwhelmingly so?" Jarak asked.

"No. With time, I can adapt to them," I conceded.

"I'm glad to hear it. And Kathleen? How does she feel about you?" Jarak asked.

I hesitated, which made him frown. "She cares for me. When

we're together, everything is perfect. She would have preferred a Black man as a mate but refused to let me design a new body accordingly," I said, before carefully choosing my words. I wanted to depict the situation accurately, and not make my woman look bad. "Kathleen likes the appearance I chose and insists that she likes me for who I am, not for how she could reshape me."

"That is excellent," Jarak said, approvingly.

"Yes, except that changed today," I countered.

He stiffened, his luminous eyes glowing with greater intensity as he waited for me to continue. I explained what had happened from the grocery store, to our walk in the hallway, to my conversation with her at the lab. For the first time, Jarak seemed genuinely speechless.

"I am so sorry, Anders," Jarak said, his voice filled with sympathy. "I had feared you might not be a match with the human female, but I had never anticipated this possible reaction from the humans. But there is no way around that rule. You cannot hide your crown, unless you display your horns or your tail."

"And I don't want to, either," I said forcefully. "I don't care about the law. I am a proud Lyrian. My mate must accept me for what I am and be proud to claim me as hers, crown and all. That will never change, even after the ten years before full citizenship is granted."

Jarak tilted his head to the side, an odd expression settling on his features as he smiled at me. "I knew you were the perfect ambassador for Lyria in the Solar System," the Patriarch said in a soft voice. "I am so very proud of you, son."

I recoiled, taken aback by this unexpected comment.

"Proud because I'm losing my soulmate?" I asked, confused.

Jarak snorted. "No, silly boy," he replied. "Proud because, despite your tremendous empathic abilities, you have not lost your sense of self-worth. You feel too deeply, which explained your endless antics growing up. I feared that you would be among those who lose themselves in their partner. Many of your brothers would have simply locked themselves home to please her and been content to be vicariously happy through their mate."

"I expected this would be your advice to me," I said, genuinely shocked.

"No, son. Losing yourself is not the way," the Patriarch said. "Yes, you can both have a pleasant life that way, but neither of you will ever know the true bliss of the communion of two souls if you do. You believe her to be your soulmate, then you must make her embrace you fully. First, you must determine the source of her reaction. Does she believe herself superior to you?"

"No, quite the opposite," I said with conviction. "She, and many of her fellow humans, think I'm too good for her. The others have a negative perception of what I am. They think I'm just an expensive sex bot. I have been studying the psychological behavior of people with low self-esteem, as I suspected my mate to be such a person. She has clear avoidance behaviors by refusing to date, go to parties, or socialize. But she also displays hiding behaviors by pretending to be tough and not caring, and by wearing those overly large clothes. Until recently, she was always too kind to others, even those that harassed her. I believe it was to make herself more likeable. She's trying to fit in."

"It sounds to me like you have already thoroughly diagnosed the problem," Jarak said, sounding impressed. "Helping your mate overcome those issues is part of your role. What troubles you about that?"

"I tell her how perfect she is to me, but the influence of her peers is too strong," I said, frustrated. "They call her a spinster. They make her feel she's not good enough for a desirable partner, only the type of man no one else would want. She believes they think that the only way she could end up with a male that looks like me would be by buying me. My crown only confirms it to the whole world."

"Is that what they really think, or is that merely her projecting her fears onto them?" Jarak asked.

That gave me pause. "You know, now that you mention it, I felt more awe, envy, and some jealousy than actual malice from the people we met," I said pensively. "There were definitely some who thought she'd bought herself a boyfriend, but you are right. I believe she's mostly projecting. Thank you, Patriarch, for helping me clarify my thoughts."

"It is my pleasure and my duty, son," Jarak said affectionately. "Do not allow her conflicting emotions to push you to despair. Trust your instincts. Your love and support will help her gain the confidence she lacks and see how beautiful she truly is. When she lapses into those episodes of insecurity, remind yourself of the times she expressed her love for you to help you through those difficult moments."

"Thank you, Patriarch. I will keep your wise advice in mind."

I ended the communication with a newfound sense of purpose. I had found my family. I would fight for my Kathleen and our little Worf.

CHAPTER 13
KATHLEEN

Using my work equipment for personal reasons contravened the company's policies. But right now, I didn't give a shit. Considering my 'personal reasons' had just saved the experiment they'd been sinking millions of dollars in, the few credits this personal call would cost represented less than a blip in the budget. I needed advice *before* going home, and this was the only place I could talk in private.

To my relief, Clarisse was just walking out of a meeting and had some free time for me.

"Hey Kitty-Kat," Clarisse said, her warm smile fading as she took in my expression. "This is not the my-pussy-is-singing-from-having-been-so-thoroughly-fucked' face I expected to see. Something wrong?"

I snorted and started laughing but it soon got strangled in my throat while tears pricked my eyes.

"Oh, sweetie," Clarisse said with that sympathetic big sister voice that normally came with a big hug whenever I was sad. "Is it really that bad?"

"He's wonderful, Clare," I said with a trembling voice. "So amazing that I naturally had to royally fuck up."

"Oh boy. What did you do?" she asked, bracing for what would follow.

I gave her a summary of the events of the past four days, including the daily divine massages, meals, epic cuddling both while watching movies and sleeping, and the sinful kissing and petting Anders increasingly lavished on me. Aside from her clear approval of all of the above, Clarisse even displayed a bit of envy, if not jealousy. And then I explained how I screwed it all up in the space of ten minutes.

"So, no. Although it's been freshly shaved, my pussy did not get any of the thorough fucking it had been looking forward to. And now, maybe it never will," I said, the tears wanting to resurface again.

Clarisse stared at me with a mix of disbelief, anger, and disapproval.

"I don't know what I want to give you shit about first: still not fucking him after four days of sharing his bed, or that stupid stunt you pulled on the poor man!" Clarisse said with an upset mommy face.

"Well, I couldn't just jump into bed with him on day one," I said defensively.

"Why not?" Clarisse asked. "He said you were his soulmate —and those guys don't lie about that stuff. He's been walking around with a raging hard on. You've been swapping damp panties faster than an old-fashioned kettle pops corn. You're both consenting adults with no one but yourselves to do any cockblocking. What's the problem?"

Indeed, what was the problem? That little voice in the back of my head telling me that I didn't want to come across as easy or slutty? But to whom? Anders wouldn't have thought that. Did anyone else's opinion matter?

It certainly shouldn't.

I squirmed in my seat and shrugged, having no valid arguments. I'd been itching to jump his bones from day one. And yet,

I had this arbitrary number of days in my head that a couple should wait before doing the deed for it to be considered meaningful.

"If there is no problem, then get on with it already," my sister said in annoyance. "At this rate, poor Anders will need a freaking jackhammer to break through the fossilized cobwebs you've got down there."

"Clarisse!" I exclaimed, floored that my 'oh so prim and proper' sister would become so crude.

"Don't Clarisse me!" she said, this time sounding genuinely upset. "I've watched you let yourself go for years, wasting away while digging in deeper in denial. You are a beautiful, smart, and funny girl, living like a fucking hermit and dressing in potato sacks large enough to fit two sumo wrestlers, side by side."

"Oh, come on—"

"No, Kathleen!" Clarisse snapped. "I've let you get away with it long enough. I know you like I made you. This 'I-don't-care-and-don't-need-anyone' front you put up is bullshit. You're lonely. But the more time you spend living as a hermit, the deeper you fall down that rabbit hole. Granted, the eligible bachelors on Mars are a disaster, but even before that, you've been afraid to get involved because you didn't think yourself good enough for any of the 'good' guys. Now, you've got the perfect guy, and you're trying to sabotage it."

"You don't understand," I said, starting to feel a little angry myself.

"What do I not understand?" Clarisse challenged. "That Anders made you the happiest you ever thought possible, but that you're ready to throw all of that away because you fear what other people may think about you and him together?"

I opened and closed my mouth a few times, failing to find an appropriate response. She had totally nailed it in one sentence, and seen that way, it made me feel utterly stupid. And yet, where my head understood how illogical my reaction was, in the heat of the moment, my emotions had a completely different mind of their own. How could you just turn off your sensitivity to the opinion of others?

"For what it's worth," Clarisse said, taking on a softer tone, "most people are likely *not* thinking what you are, not that it matters."

"What do you mean?" I asked.

"Far more humans than you realize are aware of Lyrians. You're not because you're too busy with your games and geek stuff," my sister replied with her usual dismissive air when it came to video games—she never understood that passion. "A few months ago, one of the popular daytime soap operas featured a Lyrian character. It created quite the buzz on social media. People *wish* they could have a Lyrian. Most can't afford it, and those who can are not chosen because their aura isn't nice enough."

"How much *did it* cost you?" I asked, suddenly concerned by how extravagant a gift this had been for Clarisse.

She rolled her eyes and waved a dismissive hand. "First of all, you never ask someone how much they spent on your gift," Clarisse said in a stern voice. "If I couldn't afford it, I wouldn't have offered it to you. Second, of everything I said, *that* is what held your attention? Do you realize that the Lyrians broke ALL of their rules FOR YOU?! Because that's how much of a perfect match you were for Anders and how much he was totally smitten by you. You, Kathleen, my little spinster extraordinaire of a sister, have such a beautiful aura that they were willing to bend the rules. All that just so Anders could meet you and confirm what his heart felt the minute he saw you being your silly self on a video. And you worry about the opinion of a bunch of morons who are probably seething with envy and wishing they were you right now?"

My eyes misted again, and my throat tightened both with emotion and gratitude for my sister. I had never thought of it that way. Clarisse always saw right to the heart of things while keeping the big picture in mind. She had an almost supernatural understanding of what made people tick. No wonder she was the insanely successful lead in the biggest galactic marketing firm of our planetary system.

"I'm a knucklehead, aren't I?" I said sheepishly.

"You are," Clarisse said with a nod.

"I need to fix it," I added.

"You do," my sister acknowledged.

"I love you, sis," I said with a slightly choked voice. "Thanks for setting me straight."

"I love you, too, you brat," Clarisse said affectionately. "Now go patch things up with your man, then wrap it up with some good, old-fashioned, angry sex. That might spare you the need for a jackhammer."

I burst out laughing and shook my head at my sister before hanging up. Despite my eagerness to go home and iron things out with Anders, I needed to wrap things up here first. I trashed the varberries and removed the young Kirdies from the main vivarium. After thoroughly washing their habitat, I bathed Mirik's siblings, and then placed them back inside. To my delight, they welcomed the return of their mother as well as of their estranged sibling. They all rubbed against Mirik, sharing their scent and marking him as one of them.

The baby was not out of the woods yet, but I had faith that with the care of his mother, he would make a full recovery over the next few days. Still, not wanting to take chances, I called Milan, the junior lab assistant. He was available to come babysit them for the next few hours. He would also keep an eye on my secondary project which, thankfully, didn't need much supervision, especially at this stage. Either way, an alarm would buzz me at home should anything go awry outside working hours.

With no more excuses to delay the inevitable confrontation, I made my way home. Although I passed a few people along the way, I was too lost in thought to really pay them any attention. For the first time, the walk home felt much too short.

Heart pounding, I opened the door to my living unit, wondering what kind of welcome would greet me. The delectable scent of a home-cooked meal tickled by nose. However, the total darkness inside my quarters did not bode well. I turned on the lights and called out Anders's name. Only the half-sleepy hoot from Worf answered me.

Did Anders give up on my sorry ass?

Trying to rein in my blossoming panic, I hurried to his room and knocked. When silence greeted me again, I opened the door and almost wept with relief. He had taken his Lyrian form again and was standing inside his stasis chamber. Anders had never done that before. Normally, he just lay down on his bed with that strange teaching headset on he called a Mentor. Whatever he was currently up to, I could only pray he wasn't requesting an emergency transport to get the fuck away from the crazy human spinster.

I wanted to hug him and for him to hug me back, but now was definitely not the time. Feeling a little dejected, I dragged my feet to my bedroom to take a scalding hot shower. Aside from half-boiling me, it helped loosen some of the knots twisting my back. Too bad they came back with a vengeance the minute I started getting dressed. What I wouldn't give right now for another of Anders's heavenly massages. But I needed to earn that privilege back.

This time, I hadn't just stuck my foot in my mouth, I'd shoved it all the way past my gullet, ankle and shin included. I mentally reviewed the list of all the things that made me a sorry excuse for a girlfriend. In parallel, I also listed all the reasons that him finding my aura attractive made him a saint. As a saint, it was his moral duty to spank me back onto the path of right-eousness—a punishment I would gladly subject myself to. Plus, you didn't travel to another planetary system only to give up on the insecure idiot you'd hoped to marry after only four days and one big screw up on her part.

My heart skipped a beat when Worf's happy hooting reached me from the living room. This was the moment of truth. Taking a deep breath, I stared at my reflection in the mirror and gave myself a bit of a pep talk. The flowy, sleeveless, summer dress with African patterns my sister had sent me helped boost my shaky confidence. Although loose and comfortable, just the way I liked it, the dress was actually flattering to both my figure and my complexion, contrary to the shapeless, black or dark clothes I normally wore.

"You've got this. He's crazy about you, and you're crazy about him. Everything else is nonsense you can overcome together," I whispered to my reflection.

Lifting my chin up, I walked out of my room to find Anders filling Worf's bowl with Fudian nuggets. My little brat was always poaching food from my plate, but these nuggets ensured he got the right nutrients to grow healthy. Although the amount he ate appeared ridiculously large considering his small default size, people often forget how much more massive he truly was once inflated to his battle form. All of that needed to be fed.

Anders noticed my approach just as he was closing the box. He looked at me, his face devoid of any expression. I sensed none of his earlier anger—which was a major relief. He seemed to be waiting for me to set the tone of any conversation that would follow.

I gave him a timid smile, and he responded in kind. Worf, sitting on top of the table, his big soup bowl filled with nuggets between his legs, was staring at us. The edge of the bowl stopped right below his chin. The way he tossed a nugget into his wide mouth, his head flicking between Anders and me, you'd think he was eating popcorn while readying to enjoy the unfolding drama.

"First, I would like to thank you for your insight about the varberries," I said shyly, stopping a meter in front of Anders.

"Was it any help?" he asked with sincere curiosity.

"It more than helped," I replied with a grateful smile. "It totally worked. The entire family is reunited right now, and they are all looking after him, especially his mother. You just saved both my job and little Mirik's life. I can never thank you enough for that."

Anders's face melted in an expression of pure pleasure and pride. Damn, the man was gorgeous.

"I am so happy to hear it and to have been of assistance," he said.

"You certainly have been. There are absolutely no mentions of these spores in the botanical research Josie and I consulted when we began working on this project," I said apologetically.

"You are correct," Anders conceded. "The Screener cross-referenced all relevant works in both the Solar System and Alpha Centauri. It found that the Goraldian species has the most in-depth research material. So, I learned from them."

"I really appreciate all the trouble you went through to help me out," I said, clasping my hands nervously in front of me. "It means the world to me. And, if ever it's allowed, I would love to get my hand on the Goraldian research."

"It was my pleasure, Kathleen," Anders responded softly, before taking on a sheepish expression. "As for the research, I already ordered a full copy for you two days ago. The only reason for the delay is that it isn't available in English—or any other human language. It's currently being translated. The digital copy should arrive in the next few days, but the physical copy should take at least another week."

Once more, I felt overwhelmed by just how thoughtful and amazing he was. "You are so wonderful." I almost said 'I don't deserve you' but caught myself at the last minute. Now was not the time to say something like that.

Anders looked as embarrassed as I felt. An awkward silence

settled between us, neither seeming to know where to go from here.

"I can feel your hunger," Anders said at last. "I have made—"

"No," I interrupted. "I mean, yes, I'm getting hungry, but I won't be able to eat anything until we've… you know..." I took on a deep breath and looked him straight in the eyes. "I want to clear the air about what happened earlier."

"Okay," Anders said carefully.

Although his face had taken on a neutral expression, the tension stiffening his back was unmistakable. I wanted to believe it was a good sign that he wanted to fix this as much as I did. After all, he was still here, had cooked for me, and was looking after my little rascal.

"The first thing I want to say is that I'm sorry," I said, lifting my chin. "I was so absorbed in my own feelings that I didn't think of yours. It was never my intention to hurt or offend you. What I said was out of line, both about your right to come and go as you please, but worse still me asking you to hide your origins. It was wrong, insensitive, and flat out inappropriate. I said this before, and I repeat it again: you are absolutely gorgeous and perfect just the way you are. No one should ever make you feel like you should change your appearance to please them, least of all me."

"I accept your apology," Anders said softly. "And I especially appreciate its sincerity. Appearances mean nothing to me and my species as a whole, but my identity does. I can change and will gladly sacrifice many things for you, but not this."

I nodded slowly. "Nor should you or anyone else. The problem isn't you, it's me," I said nervously.

Anders recoiled, a hurt and crushed expression descending on his gorgeous features. "You're breaking up with me?!"

"What? No! I didn't say that!" I exclaimed, on the verge of panic.

Worf hooted and shoved another nugget into his mouth. He had no idea what we were saying, but could feel the tension between us.

"You said 'It's not you, it's me.' According to my research, humans use that phrase to try and spare the feeling of the partner they want to get rid of, even though they *do* think the partner is in fact the problem," Anders argued, a confused—and still very distressed—expression on his face. "Am I the problem?"

"No! No! No! That's not it at all," I said, shaking both hands in front of me. "You're right that humans normally use that sentence exactly the way you described." Anders gaped at me with a stricken expression. "But I am not!" I added quickly. "Right here, right now, I genuinely mean that 'I' am the problem. You did nothing wrong."

"Who cares who is or isn't the problem," Anders said in an irritated voice. "You still want to send me away."

"Oh my God, no! Nobody is talking about breaking up. Stop talking about breaking up. I don't want to break up. Sheesh! You're the best thing that has ever happened to me. I'm trying to say that I fucked up, and I'm sorry, and I *don't* want to lose you," I exclaimed, feeling both annoyed and freaked out.

Anders studied my features, tension bleeding out of his shoulders before he gave me a goofy kind of smile.

"You mean it," he said to himself, sounding stunned. "Your emotions don't lie. You really mean it."

"Yes! I do mean it! So, can you please let me finish my thought without bringing up breaking up again? It's freaking me out," I said, running nervous fingers through my hair.

"Okay. Apologies," Anders said with a sheepish smile.

"So, like I was saying," I said, rolling my shoulders to release some of the tension building up there, "the problem is me —my insecurities. Humans are pretty big with that. If we don't have a reason to be insecure, we invent one. I never thought someone like you would ever want someone like me. So, the masochist in me is looking everywhere for signs confirming it was too good to be true. We're also very vulnerable to peer pressure and other people's opinions."

I shifted uncomfortably on my feet while carefully choosing my words.

"I know that appearance means nothing to you, but it does—too much—for humans. I'm considered a Plain Jane. Therefore, a handsome man like you shouldn't be 'wasted' on someone like me. I am overreaching by being with you," I explained. "And yet, if I'd been a super hot babe with you, they'd still be complaining. Except, this time, they'd be saying that I was thinking myself too hot, and too good for humans," I added, rolling my eyes.

Anders snorted and shook his head in disbelief. Yeah, we humans could be an interesting breed at times.

"People will always find something to criticize. Even 'perfect' people get gossiped over. My head knows it's wrong, but humans don't have switches to silence dumb emotions," I said, rubbing my nape. "I've always prided myself for being a rebel, impervious to peer pressure. I thought myself tougher, but I'm apparently not."

I sighed heavily again and took a couple of steps towards him.

"I don't want you to remain cooped up in here or to change who you are. But if you're willing to give me another chance, I'm definitely going to fuck up plenty of times along the way—because that's the one thing I'm really good at. But I'll eventually get there and be the best girlfriend you could ever dream of."

"I don't want a girlfriend. I want a mate," Anders deadpanned.

"I can be that, too?" I added with a small voice.

"Then I can live with that," Anders said with a smile.

Relief flooded through me.

"I really am crazy about you, Anders," I reiterated forcefully. "How I react to other people's opinion is *my* burden to learn to discard. Unfortunately, you're an Empath. That means I can't hide those stupid emotions from you. I only ask that you bear with me while I work through it."

"I will not just bear with you Kathleen," Anders said, closing the distance between us and cupping my face in his hands. "I will cure you of the cause of your insecurity. I will remind you daily that in the hundreds of Seekers that were presented to me, I refused all of them until I saw you. I CHOSE you, Kathleen, only you, because you made my heart sing. You are the most beautiful woman I have ever met—Mr. Pudge and Chewie included," he added casting an amused glance at my left big toe. "I will teach you to love yourself as much as I love you. The opinion of others won't matter then."

"I can live with that," I said, echoing his words.

He grinned and pressed his forehead to mine. "Boop," he said before kissing my lips.

After feeding my woman, I had no problem talking her into a massage. However, as soon as I began, I partially regretted it; touching Kathleen was too exciting for this body. Granted, I had learned to keep myself in check despite the almost painful erection that had become a semi-permanent state for me. But before tonight, my mate had never so loudly broadcast her desire for me to take things to the next level. Whatever soul searching she had done after our confrontation in her lab, Kathleen had decided that now, she was all in.

I should be rejoicing, but I was terrified. Kathleen's hold on me was too powerful. Patriarch Jarak hadn't been wrong by saying I felt too deeply. Once I became intimate with my woman, there would be no going back—*truly* no going back. In many ways, I had already reached the point of no return, but I wasn't bonded. I didn't think I'd be able to keep myself from doing so once we were physically joined.

What if she changes her mind after that?

Obviously, I couldn't force Kathleen to keep me. If she truly wanted me gone, I would have no choice but to comply. Staying with someone who only expressed resentment at your presence would be excruciating. No matter how well they tried to hide it, you couldn't fool an Empath.

But living without her would be just as horrible. Bonding created a physical, mental link with our partner. While it made us immune to emotional influence from other individuals we encountered or worked with, it also doubled our capacity to feel, so that we could embrace and process the full spectrum of our mate's emotions. Without her, it would become an endless void that slowly gnawed at the Empath, gradually driving him insane. Only stasis or a radical medical intervention could give him peace.

Despite that, my deepest instincts told me Kathleen would keep me. Her blossoming feelings for me were genuine. I had dreaded our conversation once she came back home. I hadn't known what to expect, but certainly not such an honest and introspective reaction from her. Instead, I had prepared myself for a potential denial of any wrong on her part, or demands from her that I be more cooperative. After all, people often had a skewed perception of Empaths. Many believed us to merely be doormats, with no personality of our own, and whose personal desires could simply be overwritten by a wish from our partner.

But not my Kathleen. She was so perfect. And she liked me as I was.

Something settled within me as these thoughts crossed my mind. Kathleen was my soulmate. I had felt it from the moment that silly video of her call with her sister had played on my screen. I took a huge risk coming here to answer the pull of my heart. I would take this risk, caution be damned. I'd take a few days of bliss with my true love—even if it meant paying the ultimate price—over an eternity of wondering what might have been.

She was worth it, and so much more...

"Turn onto your back, love," I said softly.

I felt her surprise and excitement upon hearing my words. This was the fourth massage I was giving her. Not once in the three previous times had I made her turn to face me. Normally, a full body massage required working on both sides. But we had both known doing so would take things further than we were ready for—or rather, than Kathleen was ready for. I had been ready from the moment I'd stepped out of my stasis chamber that very first day. In truth, that was usually how it went for my brothers and their Seeker. Five seconds after the initial hello, they jumped right into the horizontal dance.

Thankfully, I had only given Kathleen a Zulopian massage. Unlike the previous ones, this massage relaxed my mate without making her excessively languid. Truth be told, the others had been my shameful—and rather underhanded—way of having my Kathleen at my mercy. With her limbs feeling like jelly, she'd had no choice but to let me cradle her in my arms while she slowly emerged from her state of semi-torpor—not that she'd complained in the least.

A wave of self-consciousness rose from my mate. Although she attempted to squash it, it resonated loud and clear with my empathic abilities. At first, I couldn't see why. Granted, humans were a little shy about showing specific parts of their anatomy naked. Breasts, pubic area, and behind for females. And yet, by human standards, Kathleen's breasts were magnificent. Round and perky, the darker areola around her hard nipples made my fingers twitch with the need to touch them, and my mouth water with the urge to lick them.

I adjusted the towel on her, lowering it as much as possible below her navel, without uncovering her 'naughty' parts— another odd expression humans used. Kathleen stiffened and all but held her breath. It was baffling as I'd made it a point to grope Mr. Pudge frequently so that she would stop being self-conscious about it. However, it had been through her shirt. Having me seeing it was clearly challenging her comfort zone. I suspected her discreet stretch marks only made it worse, which was completely silly. That, too, she would have to get over.

I leaned forward and bumped my forehead on her stomach. "Boop," I said, before licking a couple of her stretch marks.

She giggled, then shivered, a mix of relief, gratitude, and awe swirling around her. Straightening, I poured a bit more massage oil on my hands before starting to apply it over her stomach, giving Mr. Pudge and her love handles a good rub until Kathleen stopped emitting those ridiculous waves of self-consciousness. My palms then ventured up her stomach to those glorious breasts she adamantly refused to keep confined in a bra the minute she got home. Usually, that part of the anatomy was not erotic for Alpha Centauri species. But my human body very much liked *boobies*, and my woman clearly enjoyed having them fondled.

"Do you know how beautiful you are, Kathleen?" I asked while my thumbs rubbed the hard nubs of her nipples.

"In your eyes, I'm starting to believe that it's quite a bit," she whispered, the shakiness of her voice stemming from both shyness and arousal.

"No, my love. Not quite a bit, but infinitely. And my eyes, and yours, are the only ones that matter," I whispered back before leaning down to kiss her.

She immediately responded, and her fingers sank into my hair. I would never tire of this kissing thing. The softness of Kathleen's plump lips against mine, her sweet taste as my tongue caressed hers, the way she always sought to get closer to me as if she wanted us to merge, to become one... each one was as addictive as the next.

My hand freely roamed over her body while I devoured her mouth, growing increasingly bolder until I brushed aside the towel that covered her pelvic area, making it fall to the floor. For the first time today, Kathleen had come to me fully naked, only wrapped in a towel instead of wearing panties for the massage.

I broke the kiss to lock gazes with my mate. Despite her underlying nervousness, her emotions screamed for me to proceed, as did the smoldering look in her eyes. Straightening, I poured a bit more massaging oil in my palm before moving down to tend to her legs. I bit the inside of my cheeks so as not to smile as Kathleen's disappointment slammed into me.

If she only knew just how badly I wanted to drag her to my room and have my way with her. And yet, a sadistic side of me I never knew existed wanted to prolong our mutual torture for a short while longer. I made it a point to not directly stare at or even touch her shaven sex, even when I slipped my hand between her thighs to part her legs a little wider.

Drawing from every single sexual massage technique I knew —and they were numerous—I made sure to massage each of the erogenous pressure points they had identified. Over the past few days, I had secretly tested which ones worked on the human anatomy while cuddling with Kathleen. Sure enough, her state of arousal skyrocketed even though my touch remained innocent in appearance.

By the time I was massaging the sole of her feet, Kathleen's legs were trembling, and she was softly moaning. I wrapped my hands around her ankles before dragging her down the massage table towards me. My mate gasped, and she looked at me through hooded eyes. Lips parted, she breathed in quick, short gasps, anticipation and a burning desire swirling around her.

Eyes locked with hers, I gently caressed the sides of her sex with both hands before gently parting her glistening petals. Kathleen's breathing picked up a notch while the delicate scent of her musk tickled my nose. I shifted on my feet to release some of the tension in my groin as her potent arousal flowing through me made me painfully hard.

A violent tremor ran through my mate as my fingers gently

teased the seam of her sex, while continuing to avoid her clitoris. Bowing down, I lifted one of her legs dangling at the edge of the table, and kissed her inner thighs before gently nipping at it. The organic—and especially edible—massaging oil had a surprisingly pleasant taste, combined with the slight saltiness of my woman's skin. Kathleen emitted a strangled sound followed by an even deeper moan when I slipped two of my fingers inside her.

My lips slowly worked their way up the apex of her thighs while the movement of my hand inside her accelerated. My mate's inner walls contracting around my fingers made my cock throb with need. Letting her leg rest on my shoulder, I fleetingly licked Kathleen's engorged little nub. She cried out, her back arching off the table and her legs shaking violently. There was something intoxicating about being able to so easily take my mate to the edge. By the time the night ended, I wanted Kathleen completely mad for me.

Finally putting an end to her torment, only to subject her to a different one, I sucked her clit into my mouth. At the same time, I curved my fingers upward inside her to target her G-spot. Kathleen shouted my name and lifted her pelvis so abruptly that she'd likely have broken my nose had I not lifted my head when I did.

Note to self: my mate becomes a health hazard when she climaxes.

While my fingers continued to torment her sensitive spot, I placed my free hand on her stomach, holding her down before resuming my feast. Both of Kathleen's hands held on to my hair with the fierceness of a cowboy holding the reins of a bucking bronco during a rodeo. The sting to my scalp might have been unpleasant if I hadn't been drowning in the waves of ecstasy pouring out of my mate. That merely my fingers and my mouth could make my mate come so hard had me feeling like a god among mortals.

As she began to come down from her high, the need to make

her fly again burned within me with a vengeance. I couldn't say if that hunger stemmed more from me than her, but it was definitely a mix of both.

However, this table was much too narrow and kept me from fully enjoying my woman. Without stopping feasting on my mate, I slid down my shorts—to my confined cock's utter relief—and kicked them off along with my slippers. Letting Kathleen's leg off my shoulder, I straightened long enough to all but rip my shirt off, before picking her up in my arms.

Still trembling from the aftermath, she wrapped her arms around my neck and her legs around my waist. Pressed against the burning heat of her stomach, my cock throbbed with anticipation while liquid fire bubbled in my nether region. Drunk with lust, I captured her lips in a searing kiss while carrying her to my room. An alarmed hoot from Worf indicated I'd almost trampled him as I blindly led my bride to my lair. The Fudian wisely sought refuge elsewhere, guessing now wasn't the time to cuddle with us.

Still kissing my woman, I entered my bedroom and kicked the door shut behind me. By the time I laid Kathleen down on my bed, the sexual frenzy that had been raging within me appeared to have taken her over. My mate all but forced me onto my back. Her hands and mouth were everywhere at once, caressing, clawing, kissing, licking, and nipping my flesh like it was the greatest treat. Each touch left a burning trail on my skin that had my abdominal muscles contracting.

But beyond the carnal pleasure of my woman's touch, her emotions were utterly wrecking me. No words could express the awe and feral hunger Kathleen felt for me and for my body. The way she explored me like she couldn't believe I was hers, the possessiveness of her hands on me, the adoration and passion with which she claimed me made me want to lose myself in her forever. When her hands wrapped around my cock, I almost died with pleasure. I'd ached for this from the moment I'd felt the beauty of her aura.

In all of my years on Lyria, I had often dreamed of the species I would become. Never in a million years would I have imagined it to be a human, and least of all guessed at the wonders of their coupling. For most species of Alpha Centauri, mating only served for reproduction, not pleasure or bonding. Love, affection, and intimacy were expressed in different ways that conveyed tenderness, not this all-consuming passion.

But I blissfully surrendered to my mate as her greedy hands gave way to the blistering heat of her mouth closing all around my length. I cried out Kathleen's name while savagely fisting the blankets. An inferno raged in my groin, threatening to erupt any minute as my woman bobbed over me. I had never thought such an intense pleasure possible. I didn't believe myself strong enough to last very long, and yet, I couldn't bring myself to make her stop. My selfish need kept me pinned in place, writhing with pleasure under my mate's ministrations. But the sense of triumph and pride soaring within Kathleen in light of the powerful effect that her touch had on me only reinforced my desire to abandon myself to her.

However, the moment she had me on the verge of toppling over, something snapped inside of me. I grabbed Kathleen's shoulders and yanked her away from my groin before forcing her onto her back. Despite the sliver of disappointment that emanated from her for being deprived of making me fall apart as I had done to her, excitement and a burning anticipation shone even brighter within my mate.

"You're mine," I growled with an angry possessiveness as I spread her open and lay on top of her.

I had meant to be gentle, to carefully insert myself inside my woman, to gently bring her to the edge of ecstasy before making her soar on the endless wings of bliss. Instead, I rammed myself home in one powerful thrust. Despite how wet she'd been for me, and how I'd prepared her to receive me on the massage table, Kathleen was excruciatingly tight. It hurt so fucking good.

She cried out, her pain echoing mine. And yet, she spurred me on, urging me to keep going, and to give it to her hard. I didn't hold back. Kathleen's nails dug into my back as she spread her legs even wider so that I could take her deeper, harder. Her moans of pleasure-pain mingled with mine, the furiously slapping sound of our flesh meeting, and the whining of the bed under my unbridled assault. Ancestors! Her sex gripping mine, squeezing me in its burning vise, and stroking me with each thrust was slowly killing me.

I bent down to crush her lips with a kiss. Something in the way I'd moved had struck Kathleen's sweet spot. The explosion of pleasure she projected towards me nearly undid me. But I wouldn't climax before her, in spite of the lava boiling in my gut. Without slowing down my punishing pace, I shifted my angle until my mate emitted that strangled cry again, and that bolt of pleasure she felt echoed inside me.

I pummeled it relentlessly while devouring her mouth. Her orgasm struck her so hard, her back arched off the mattress, and she froze, her lips opened in a silent O. Kathleen's inner walls clamping down on my cock undid me. Lightning struck the base of my spine, and I threw my head back with a powerful roar. A blinding light exploded before my eyes while my human seed erupted in a blissful flow into my woman.

Kathleen collapsed beneath me, her body shaking with spasms of ecstasy. I felt faint, my skin tingling and my head spinning. And yet, with a will of their own, my hips kept pumping in and out of my mate until the last of my seed was spent.

Boneless, I let myself fall on top of my mate. Body slick with sweat, my labored breath and pounding heart echoing hers, I felt too weak to move. By who knew what miracle, I managed to summon enough strength to roll off my Kathleen and draw her against me. Laying on my back, I stared at the ceiling without seeing it while my mind floated in a sea of ecstasy—both mine and my mate's.

I was blissfully wrecked, and irrevocably in love with my human.

CHAPTER 15
ANDERS

That night, after five more rounds, a couple of showers, and two changes of bedsheets, we both fell into a blissful sleep. None of my learnings about human courtship and sex had prepared me for how messy this whole thing could get. I didn't really mind it, but it had a way of ruining the mood when you just wanted to cuddle but felt much too sticky.

After yet another round in the morning, we had to scramble a bit to get Kathleen dressed and fed in time to go to work. Granted, no one would have given her an earful for being a little late this once, but my mate took great pride in always being reliable and on time.

We still managed to sit down at the table to eat under Worf's very judgmental glare. We hadn't exactly been quiet. On a couple of occasions during the night, he had expressed his disapproval as our shouting had startled him out of his slumber.

I almost felt bad. Almost…

"So…," Kathleen said after swallowing a bite of her toast with a much too thick layer of peanut butter on it. "We miraculously didn't wreck the furniture last night, but we didn't speak about contraception."

Although she said it nonchalantly, and tried to make it humorous, Kathleen was serious about this. The question of offspring was normally handled as part of the initial screening. In the form she'd filled out on Kathleen's behalf, Clarisse stated that her sister would eventually want multiple kids, but not necessarily right away. With their advances in medicine and increase in the overall lifespan of their species, human females could now easily conceive healthy children up to the age of fifty-seven. As she was only thirty-six, that still gave us a little over twenty-years to have a family.

"I cannot impregnate you as long as we aren't bonded," I said in a gentle voice. "While my current appearance is human, with all of its functions, my DNA remains Lyrian. My people cannot reproduce with other species unless we 'become' them. We are incompatible. So, as you humans say, for now I shoot blanks. Messy blanks, but blanks nonetheless."

She snorted and nodded slowly. "And when we're bonded?" she asked.

My heart leapt at her choice of word. "*When* we're bonded?" I repeated. "Not *if?*"

A flash of uncertainty crossed her beautiful brown eyes. To my relief, lack of self-confidence and not second guesses about us had triggered it. While that still needed to be fixed, it reassured me about us.

"Well, considering your phenomenal performance last night and this morning, I can definitely say that we're totally headed towards a *when* and not an *if*," she said, trying to sound cocky and naughty to hide her timidity.

I puffed out my chest, very pleased with myself. "I'm happy to hear it, because I have no intentions of letting you go," I answered sincerely. "As for your question, after we are bonded, it will be up to you. I would love a family with you. If and when that happens will entirely be your decision—after all, you will be the one carrying those babies. Until then, if you do not wish to take contraceptives, we have our own. It is natural with no short-term or long-term side-effects. I will be glad to take it if you wish."

"You know, you really need to stop being so perfect," Kathleen said as if I'd done something wrong once too many. "It's not even fair for other men. Guys usually balk at anything that could affect the functioning of their plumbing, but have no problem whatsoever making us mess with ours."

"Are you sure you wish me to stop being 'perfect'?" I teased.

"Nope! I totally want you to stay as you are," she quickly amended, making me chuckle. "I have to go," she added, rising to her feet with a wince. "Ugh. Who would have thought having wild, raunchy sex was such a work out? I can't remember the last time I've had so many sore muscles. You'd think I'd just had an intense Iron Man training."

This time, I burst out laughing. I could totally relate. Dozens of muscles I didn't even know I possessed were whining at having been so brutally and unexpectedly exerted.

"Speaking of which," I said, carefully while also rising to my feet, "my own muscles have made me realize they need a bit more activity. I understand there is an excellent gym on the station?"

I left the words hanging between us. Before entering semi-stasis after puberty, I had been a very active male. I naturally hungered for frequent physical activity. Furthermore, the sexy, fitness model body I currently possessed would benefit from such training. Before natural ageing started taking its toll on me, I wanted to maintain that superb body for my woman to keep drooling over.

I hadn't specified when I wanted to start using the gym, leaving the door open for Kathleen to suggest a timeline that would be easier for her to handle in light of her insecurity hang ups. Still, my heart swelled with pride as the echoes of my empathic abilities picked up her efforts to quell the wave of self-consciousness rising within her.

Kathleen lifted her chin in defiance to herself and looked me straight in the eyes. "The gym is not too far from my lab. If you can get ready quickly enough, I could show you on my way to work," she said firmly. "There's also a really beautiful atrium nearby. It has a bar with both alcoholic and non-alcoholic beverages, snacks, light meals, a reading area, and a virtual reality movie screening section. If you decide to make use of any of them, put everything on my tab."

I opened my mouth to argue about that last part, but she continued quickly to cut me off.

"All these services are free for employees and their partners. And I get a *huge* employee discount on food. It's part of the perks to con us into coming to live on Mars," she added with a shrug.

"And you say I am the one who is too perfect?" I asked softly. I smiled at the timid expression that descended on her face. "I love you for leaving the door wide open for me. But there is no pressure, Kathleen. It doesn't have to be all or nothing."

She shook her head, her face taking on a mulish expression. "If you want to learn how to swim, you need to get your ass in the pool. Dipping your toes in the water from the side will not get you anywhere," she said with conviction. "I hate that my stupid brain continues to worry about what other people will think, but it's going to learn who's the boss—and that's me. We have nine days left for me to prove to you that you didn't make a mistake by taking such a huge leap of faith on my sorry ass. I'm not going to waste them."

I came to stand next to Kathleen.

"You have nothing to prove," I said softly, cupping her lovely face in my hands. "I was yours the moment I felt your aura. Last night only sealed it."

"Yes, I do," Kathleen argued, wrapping her fingers around my wrists, her thumbs gently caressing the back of my hands. "You may not need me to prove it to you, but I need to prove it to myself. I want to see myself the way you do. I don't just want to have you. I want my brain to accept that I also deserve you. And then I want to make all those hot bitches on the station go green with jealousy because they'll never get as perfect a partner —and indefatigable a sex machine—as my own little Lyrian."

I wanted to chuckle, but a growl came out instead as blood rushed to my groin. How could I still be so hungry for her? Kathleen was the one to chuckle instead.

"Someone's getting horny," she teased, letting go of one of my wrists to rub my crotch. "Too bad we don't have time."

"That expression is silly," I grumbled, pressing her hand even harder on my groin to increase the friction. "Lyrians naturally have horns, and I can assure you that we do not walk around in a constant state of arousal."

She laughed, but it quickly died under my lips claiming hers, and my tongue demanding entry. It took every ounce of my willpower not to drag her back to my room, or toss her onto the couch to have my way with her.

"Damn you, female. You're my drug," I growled against her lips.

"Well, your drug is about to be late in administering some to her subjects," she said teasingly. "So, hurry up and cover that sexy bubble butt of yours so that I can flaunt you around the base on my way to work."

"Your will is my command," I said, brushing my lips against hers one last time before hurrying to my room.

As I had not brought proper training clothes—the hidden compartment of my stasis chamber having contained only the strict minimum to function—I intended to buy all that I needed. It was the Lyrians' preferred approach since fashion differed greatly from one culture to the next. Today, considering how sore

I felt after my vigorous romps with Kathleen, I was probably going to take it easy, but would still welcome a reconnaissance tour of the gym and around the base.

I decided to make a quick stop by the bathroom to relieve my bladder. To my dismay, on top of having no control over my body's responses to my mate, I discovered that trying to pee with a stiff cock was quite the acrobatic feat. Trying to aim downwards when all it wanted was to point up had me all but hovering horizontally over the toilet.

Kathleen calling out my name from the living room made me realize how much time I'd wasted trying to accomplish what should have taken seconds. I quickly washed my hands while cursing under my breath. Still, in spite of the inconveniences, I couldn't hate on what gave me so much pleasure while being one with my mate. I donned one of my three 'respectable' outfits so that I could traipse around outside, and hurried back out of the room.

She gave me a questioning look when I finally emerged.

As I scrunched my face, it dawned on me that I was imitating one of the expressions Kathleen made whenever she got caught doing something she shouldn't.

"Trying to pee with a hard on is a rather taxing experience," I mumbled apologetically. "I do not recommend it."

Kathleen burst out laughing and shook her head at me. "I will take your word on it. Just tell me you didn't paint the walls yellow."

My outraged expression must have said it all because she laughed again and raised her palms in an appeasing gesture.

"Just checking!" she said teasingly. "Don't get your panties in a bunch! Now, come on, slowpoke. I'm late!"

"I don't wear panties," I mumbled while she leaned down to kiss Worf's head.

She took my hand and then pulled me after her out of the living unit. Although we didn't meet anyone in the first couple of corridors leading from the residential quarters to the indus-trial sector, Kathleen's stress steadily grew. It struck me then that her fear had somewhat shifted from what other people would think to how I would respond to whatever her reaction would be once we ran into other people. It pleased me to the extent that it implied she was letting go of the core issue I wanted to help her with: not letting other people's influence impact her behavior.

Then again, it could be said that she had only traded worrying about the opinion of the masses to stressing out about mine. But I would be an easier hurdle for her to overcome.

However, the minute we entered the industrial sector, bustling activity greeted us.

"Woah!" I said, watching all the people manning a series of lifts carrying heavy crates. Each of them was filing one behind the other with apparently the same destination. "It wasn't that busy yesterday."

"It's the warehouse staff," Kathleen explained. "They are bringing the last of the Christmas party stuff to the reception hall. Frankly, I'm surprised they are working on it so last minute. Usually, Patty is almost two weeks too early and ends up changing ideas a billion times. I bet the warehouse staff lost it on her having them move the same things around fifty-times," she added with a chuckle.

"I see," I replied, as we entered a different corridor from the one they were taking.

To my relief, despite the many stares our way, the emotions I perceived from the people around us were merely curiosity at a novelty. Some broadcast admiration, which I believed aimed at my mate for 'catching' me.

"Speaking of which," Kathleen said, looking suddenly super nervous, "I had planned on boycotting the party this year. But now, I'm thinking it would be a great thing for you to experience a corporate Christmas party. Would you like to go? Which also means you'll be stuck with me as your date," she added with an even more nervous laughter.

The strong fear of rejection emanating from her saddened me. She clearly had no skills at inviting a man out on a date. Still, it meant the world to me that she had put herself out there and taken a risk, even though she should know better as far as I was concerned.

"I would love the honor of being your date should you decide to attend," I replied. "I promise to eat with my mouth closed, not to step on your toes when we dance, and not to knock out any men who look at your beauty with a bit too much insistence."

She gave me a playful tap and made a face at me. "You never eat with your mouth open, silly man," she said. "And it's your toes you should be worried about. I'll be the one stomping all over them. You also shouldn't have too many men to knock out, maybe aside from Wilson who will be pissed you scored the spinster that denied him. But I make no promises not to slap the bitches that drool a little too close to you."

I chuckled, and opened my mouth to respond when a wave of tension rose from Kathleen. My gaze followed hers and landed on a group of three: two females and a male. They were staring at my mate with the kind of smile that rubbed me the wrong way. The 'Alpha' female of the group, in particular, emitted the type of malicious jealousy one would expect from a bully. It was all the more disturbing that she would qualify as a beautiful woman by human standards. So, why would she begrudge Kathleen her 'good fortune' in finding a mate?

"Well, well, nice pet you've got there," the female said while giving me a lurid glance. "You must be dead broke now."

The anger flaring inside of me echoed the one emanating from my woman.

"He's not a pet, he's my man, and I didn't pay for him," Kathleen said in an icy cold voice, while slipping her hand through mine. "But yes, he's beyond nice. You should try it, for a change." While the female gasped, my mate turned to look at the stunned man accompanying her. "When you walk your bitch in public spaces, you're supposed to keep her on a leash."

I burst out laughing, before immediately forcing myself to stop, although I couldn't wipe the proud—if not evil—grin from my face. Without giving them a chance to recover from their shock and outrage, my woman led me away by the hand.

By their flabbergasted expression, I guessed her response had been as unexpected to them as it had been to me. I doubted Kathleen had ever talked back that way in the past. She was more the type to ignore it and keep walking: not feeding the bully but also not calling them out. I was glad she had given the warning shot not to mess with her.

Despite my urge to give the 'bitch' a piece of my mind, I didn't want to steal Kathleen's thunder. I squeezed her hand to express my approval the minute I felt the mortification emanating from her. She shouldn't feel embarrassed for standing up for herself.

"Sorry," she mumbled, casting me a sideways glance.

"Are you kidding?" I said with a grin. "That was an awesome takedown," I added, hiding none of the pride I felt. "Don't you dare feel bad. She was trying to embarrass you out of pure spite and jealousy. She deserved that tongue lashing. And you were nicer than I would have been."

Kathleen's head jerked towards me, and she stared at me with bulging eyes.

I chuckled. "My love, being an Empath doesn't mean being sweet and angelic," I explained. "There are jerks, bullies, and self-centered assholes among my people as well. It is less frequent because our empathic abilities make it hard for the majority to take pleasure in the pain of innocents when you also feel every single bit of it. But the same way punching a jerk in the face—or kicking him in the nuts as you humans seem quite fond of—can be quite liberating, being able to enjoy every nuance of the emotional distress you inflict to a bully can be quite orgasmic. And distressed, 'the bitch' was."

Kathleen burst out laughing. "Okay, I can see that. I still feel bad," she added, scrunching her face in that adorable way of hers. "I don't like being mean to people. But I don't regret saying what I did. Myrna can pick on me if she wants, but I won't put up with anyone disrespecting you."

That further melted my heart. At the grocery store, I'd been too distraught by her seething anger to pay much attention when she had bitten the cashier's head off for leering at me. In retrospect, even then and despite the humiliation she felt, Kathleen had been protective of me.

"You are so incredibly perfect," I whispered, my throat tightening.

She smiled timidly, her face heating as she stole a glance at me.

"Find a room, you two," a young man leading a hovercart laden with containers called out as he walked past us with a grin. "You're going to make the entire base overheat!"

I chuckled, while Kathleen made a face at him, her cheeks taking on a pinkish hue beneath her golden skin. Letting go of her hand, I instinctively wrapped an arm around her shoulders. I hadn't meant to so openly display our relationship and immediately kicked myself for my impulsive action. To my relief, Kathleen slipped her arm around my waist and lifted her chin defiantly. My mate still had a ways to go in building her self-confidence, but she had indeed jumped into that pool headfirst. I couldn't have been prouder.

However, the last thing I expected when we entered the gym was to come face to face with Wilson.

Kathleen's tension skyrocketed the minute she caught a glimpse of her suitor adjusting the weights on one of the machines. Judging by the panic on her face and the anxiety she felt, my mate was dying to drag me right out of the gym before

Wilson could see us. But, as if that thought had called him, the muscular male's head turned toward us. His eyes widened, lingering on me before settling on my mate with a betrayed expression.

But it was the flurry of emotions swirling within him that held my attention. They spoke a completely different discourse than the one etched on his face.

"I will talk to him," Kathleen offered nervously.

"About what?" I asked in a surprised tone. "Were you in some sort of a relationship with him that would require you to clear the air?"

"Of course, not," Kathleen said as if I'd said something ludicrous. "But..."

"But nothing," I said when her voice trailed off. "You are not responsible for his feelings. You have been honest with him from the start. Talking to him would imply you owe him an explanation. You don't."

Her shoulders slumped. "You're right. But I don't want him giving you a hard time. He's not a bad guy. It's just that his mouth, logic, and tact all oscillate on conflicting wavelengths," she explained as if she was speaking of an alien species that defied logic. "Occasionally, he can be a total jerk—often in fact. But I doubt he even realizes just how offensive he comes across sometimes. So, if he pesters you, please keep that in mind, okay? I would rather you not kick his ass with one of your hundreds of alien combat techniques. He's taken enough blows lately."

I chuckled, my heart warming further for my mate. "Do not fear, my love. I have no intentions of breaking his poor soul further. After all, I got the girl," I said smugly.

She snorted and smiled shyly. "That, you most certainly did."

"Go on, my beauty. You don't want to be late for work," I said before gently kissing her lips.

She nodded and forced herself not to look in his direction. I hated the anxiety still bubbling inside her as she left, but that couldn't be helped. As soon as the door closed behind her, I ignored the trainer stepping out of his windowed office with a welcome smile and made a beeline for Wilson instead. He stiffened, straightening with a defiant air like an alpha male preparing to defend his territory against another roaming alpha.

"If you're coming here to gloat," Wilson said preemptively as I closed the distance between us, "you're wasting your time."

"I'm not," I said, stopping just outside of his personal space. "But my soulmate was worried things might get ugly between us since I intend to make regular use of these facilities."

He snorted. "Soulmate? She fucking bought you!" he argued.

"No," I said, slowly shaking my head. "You cannot 'buy' a Lyrian. I *chose* her. Kathleen didn't even know about me until I showed up on her doorstep. The fees linked to mating with one of us are purely administrative, similar to those incurred during international adoption."

"Yeah, well, whatever. I don't care," Wilson said dismissively.

My face softened as I looked at the human.

"You are a handsome male by human standards, successful in your career, very smart according to your professional profile, and you actually have a rather pleasant aura," I reflected out loud, genuinely surprised by the latter. "Women should be falling at your feet."

Wilson stiffened, confusion and a quickly dissimulated flicker of sadness replacing the defiant expression on his face.

"On my home world, we all look alike," I continued, clasping my hands behind my back. "Our features are so undefined we wouldn't be able to distinguish each other if not for our ability to perceive auras. Personality is all that matters for us. Humans are quite different. Judging by your obsession with fitness, I'm speculating you have been severely hurt because of your appearance when you were younger."

His surge of emotion and the sharp pain that coursed through him confirmed I had hit the nail on the head.

"You don't know what you're talking about, and I don't need you to try and psycho-analyze me. You got the girl, congrats! Now piss off," Wilson snarled.

I smiled but didn't budge one iota. "Whatever scarred you in your past, let it go. Just like my Kathleen has been hiding behind her oversized clothes, you are hiding behind your muscles and your cocky attitude," I said in a soft voice. "You pursue the so-called 'Plain Janes' and 'Spinsters' because they are easy prey, and because each success reinforces your impression of being good enough."

"I said piss off," Wilson growled, taking one menacing step towards me.

I smiled again with sympathy, feeling his walls crumbling despite his efforts to cling on to them.

"You have a beautiful soul, Wilson," I said, ignoring his threat. "And you're no longer the ugly duckling. Act like the swan you've become. Stop beating everyone's ears down about how great you think you are. Just be yourself, and they will see it. Pursue the female you truly want instead of just the ones you think you can win. And then listen to her. The secret to capturing the heart of the one you want is simply listening and paying attention to her. She will always end up saying what she really needs for you to win her heart."

On these last words, I nodded at him then turned around to go meet the trainer who was looking at us with a slightly alarmed expression. We had been too far away for him to hear our discussion, but our body language had hinted at the tension. Still, it was Wilson's emotions I focused on. His anger and sense of betrayal had given way to confusion as he mulled over my words. But the one underlying emotion emanating from him that made me smile was a timid spark of hope.

CHAPTER 16
KATHLEEN

The next few days leading up the Christmas party were beyond magical. I still felt self-conscious anytime someone brought up Anders, even in passing. However, I now realized it wasn't so much because of the whole 'did she buy herself a boyfriend?' bullshit, but rather that I feared they were saying how I wasn't good enough for him.

Good enough or not, my insecurities could go choke on a big fat cock while I was busy riding one. There would be no jack-hammers needed for this chick; my vagina was singing arias every night… and morning. If not for work, she'd probably sing a few more times during the day as well.

But epic sex was just the icing on the cake. As part of helping me work on my self-love, Anders had also set his sights on my wardrobe. At first, I'd been ready to get all up in arms about it. I refused to wear a bra at home or any type of confining clothes ever. But, to my utter relief, Anders not only supported the no bra policy—as it gave him easier access to the girls whenever his hands got antsy—but he also shared my comfy clothes preferences.

However, after years of celibacy and 'rebellion' against the established norms, I had indeed let myself go. I'd started settling for whatever was comfortable without paying attention to how it looked on me. The loose but fashionable clothes Clarisse had sent me along with Anders had been a wakeup call and planted those first seeds of change. Wearing them and seeing how flattering they were to both my figure and my complexion made me feel good about myself. Sure, I wanted to look good for Anders, but he didn't give a shit about my appearance—only how I felt. And looking pretty made me feel wonderful, which in turn made him feel happy.

I still boycotted makeup, high heels, and fancy hairdos, but making an effort to like what I saw in the mirror rather than avoiding looking at it, did wonders for my self-esteem.

Anders was wonderful. Although he was constantly pampering me, he didn't do it just to win my affection: he genuinely enjoyed it. My man wasn't a slave or a pushover. He had a mind of his own, had no problem expressing his likes, dislikes, and preferences. And above all, he didn't hesitate to call me out on my bullshit like he had done that first time after the grocery store incident.

He adored Worf, and my little Fudian loved him right back.

And right now, my alien was looking absurdly sexy in black leather pants and a form-fitting black shirt with a single, multi-colored strip along the length of his right sleeve. It matched the palette of the fancy, tribal, maxi dress Clarisse had sent me. The neckline, without being plunging, gave a rather nice peek at my cleavage. Making a bit more effort than usual, I'd pulled my hair into a messy bun. It allowed my big, faux gauge tribal earrings to stand out as they delicately framed my face.

Anders fastened around my neck the matching spiral necklace made in a material that looked like fake horn. He then kissed my nape. I leaned back against his chest while he wrapped his arms around my midsection. And just like that, I no longer wanted to go out. I only wanted to bask in his affection, cuddle with him on my couch, and simply savor being together.

He seemed to share that feeling as he reluctantly let go of me. He made me turn around to face him before kissing the tip of my nose.

"It's time to see what kind of party Patty threw together, eat her food, step on people's toes on the dance floor, and hopefully, for me to see what kind of drunk you are," he said teasingly.

I chuckled. "I agree with all of the above, except for the drunk part," I argued. "I'm not big on alcohol. But I am eager to see how a Lyrian holds his liquor."

"I will not drink unless you do," he replied tauntingly. "So, if you want to see me drunk, you will need to lead the way."

"That's not fair!" I exclaimed with a pout. "How am I supposed to enjoy you making a spectacle of yourself if I'm already rolling under the table?"

"I'm sure Patty will record it all for posterity," Anders deadpanned. He burst out laughing at my horrified expression. Tucking me under his arm, he glanced at Worf who was sitting on the couch and chewing away at the giant foot Clarisse had sent for him. "We leave the unit in your good care. Don't set it on fire."

Worf stopped chewing long enough to hoot before resuming to gum the hell out of the toy. I shook my head affectionately and let my man lead me out to the party.

Overnight, Patty's teams had performed miracles, transforming the sleek and modern common rooms and hallways of the base into a winter wonderland. The floors were covered with some kind of white cushioned carpet that crunched under foot like freshly fallen snow. Luminous icicles and giant snowflakes lined the edges of the ceiling. In the central hub connecting the residential sector to the industrial one, Santa's Little Helper's Village had been erected with a variety of games and activities for the three dozen children who lived on the base with their parents.

As an eternal kid myself, I intended to visit it in the upcoming days, and even let Worf get on some of the small rides. Thankfully, the village would stay up until after the New Year's celebrations.

Like us, many people were converging on the reception hall. The turn out surprised me. Things had been so quiet over the past couple of weeks that I had assumed a lot less people had stayed on the base through the holidays. As Patty loved extravagant bashes, she had to be thrilled to host so many people. The mere thought of organizing a party of this magnitude made me dizzy. I was into a completely different type of masochism.

Looking around us at the crowd flooding in, I was once more impressed by how nicely the staff of a mining corporation set on Mars could clean up for a party. We might as well have been at the Oscars with all the glitz and glamour. While I certainly enjoyed gawking at the ladies in their sequined dresses, I couldn't help but wonder at the logic of paying through the nose for a dress they'd probably never wear again.

For all that, Anders and I drew plenty of attention as well. To my shock—and utterly pleasant surprise—they were all mostly friendly and admirative. The rest expressed nothing more than the usual curiosity one had about other people's outfits when on a fancy outing. I'd so dreaded how our first official public date might have gone down. The normalcy of people's behavior was not only anticlimactic, it also drove home how our minds were often our own worst enemy. I'd wasted so much energy imagining all kinds of scenarios when, in reality, people had much better things to do than worry about who one of the Xenobiologists in Sector A3 was banging at night.

We were greeted with a glass of champagne by waiters and waitresses dressed as tastefully sexy Christmas elves. One of them then ushered us to our table. We were the first there, and I couldn't deny worrying a little as to who would be the six other people joining us.

Here as well, the winter wonderland theme had been replicated. A giant silver and blue Christmas tree occupied the corner of the room, strategically placed near the exit. Around it, two-tiered tables were laden with his and hers gift bags. Cotton wool had been cleverly used to form snowbanks all around the hall. Small reindeer and polar bear figurines could be spotted here and there, peering around the fake snow. A holographic night sky covered the ceiling, with the occasional shooting star passing through it. A number of snow and ice sculptures livened the place, not to mention more of the luminous icicles and giant snowflakes.

Linda and her husband Gerald were the first to join us. He worked as a production manager whereas she supervised the quality assurance team. I always thought it had to be awkward when he was fighting to meet his minimum quotas, and she was rejecting part of his mineral shipments for not respecting quality standards. And yet, somehow, they made it work. Gerald was really eager for the successful completion of my Kirdie project as the creatures would significantly help his prospecting efforts.

Next to join us, the identical twins, Alie and Marnie, were mining whizz-kids. At twenty-eight, they jointly held the record of the greater number of most perilous drills successfully completed. They were real adrenaline junkies with whom I occasionally played team combat games. Now that I'd started roping in Anders, I was looking forward to four vs. four battle arenas. Paired with the fantastic twins, we would obliterate the competition.

We were having a friendly conversation with our table partners when Alie's sudden worried expression drew first Anders attention, and then mine. Following her gaze, my stomach dropped at the sight of Wilson casually approaching our table. To my shock, Naomi appeared to be accompanying him.

She wasn't the hottest girl on the base, but definitely qualified as a solid contender to the title. Like me, she worked in the research department, but in the engineering field. Wilson designed the most advanced mining and excavation equipment in the industry. Naomi invented and created the complex parts needed to make his vision a reality. From temperature to oxygen control at extreme depths, to laser beams and deionizers to pierce through the hardest layers of rock keeping the miners from their prize, she did it all.

What the fuck is she doing with him?

She was too smart, too poised, too great a catch to be drawn to this narcissist. Anders had told me things had been distantly cordial between him and Wilson over the past four days of him going to the gym. I suspected something had gone down between the two of them, but Anders insisted they had simply exchanged a few words to get everyone on the same page and then gone about their business.

"Hi, Naomi," I said with a warm smile as she reached our table and Wilson pulled out her chair so she could sit. "What an unexpected pleasure!"

"You mean what an unexpected shock to see such a fine lady accompanying a self-centered buffoon like me?" Wilson asked teasingly while settling down next to Naomi. They were both sitting across the table from us, Linda and Gerald on my right, and the twins on Anders's left.

Naomi snorted while I gaped at Wilson, robbed of voice. It wasn't just that he had nailed my exact thoughts on the head, but also the lack of malice or bitterness in his voice. His words had been delightfully playful and spoken in a humorously self-derisive tone.

"I wasn't going to say that," I said carefully, while not actually denying it.

Wilson chuckled, seeing right through me, which threw me

even more for a loop. "I only succeeded because I conned her into it," he said, puffing out his chest smugly.

My head jerked towards Naomi who nodded with a fatalistic smile. "He played me like a violin."

"Okay, this I've got to hear," Alie said in a tone that reflected the general curiosity around the table.

"Lately, we've been spending a lot of time working together on the Mech 3 model. I told Naomi that if I managed not to speak a word about training, fitness, or dieting, and if I didn't brag once, in any shape or form, for an entire day, she would accompany me to the party," Wilson said.

"No fucking way you won that," Gerald said before realizing what he had said.

It could have quickly turned awkward, but Naomi emitted an exaggerated long-suffering sigh, and slumped her shoulders in pretend discouragement. "I'm here, so…"

We all laughed.

Pleasantly surprised, I didn't hide my admiration as I turned to Wilson. "I'm impressed," I said sincerely. "There might be hope for you yet."

The sarcastic remark didn't come. Instead, his face softened with an unreadable expression.

"A wise man made me realize that you can reach your goals faster by listening rather than talking. Too bad it took me this long for it to sink in," Wilson said.

"Better late than never," Anders said gently. "Considering it helped you score a date with such a lovely lady, late wasn't such a bad thing after all."

We all laughed again, while Naomi's pale skin flushed. She was a beautiful Eurasian woman, with a milky skin, long black hair, and pitch-black, elongated eyes. Her long eyelashes cast a shadow over her cheeks as she timidly smiled at Anders. Lucky for her, I didn't sense any attempt at seduction. I would have hated to have to bring the smackdown on her for trying to move in on my turf.

I cast a sideways glance at Anders. He gave me an enigmatic look in return. However, the subtle way his hand resting on my lap squeezed it, appeared to confirm my suspicion that he was the 'wise man' Wilson had alluded to.

By the time dinner was served, a surprisingly pleasant atmosphere reigned around the table. Wilson was such a different man when he wasn't constantly bragging and trying to keep the attention on himself. In fact, he was getting a lot more of it by simply inquiring about other people. Naomi and he weren't a couple yet, but the way he looked at her when he thought no one was paying attention made me realize she wasn't just another conquest to him. Wilson was truly taken by Naomi. I didn't know if things would pan out between them, but if he could remain the charming man he'd been so far this evening, there might be hope.

Anders did get a number of questions about his origin, his culture, and mating into a completely foreign species. Although I'd grilled him about all of it, I still discovered new things about him.

"It must be awesome speaking so many languages, so fluently, and without the slightest accent," Marnie reflected out loud.

"It is, but that's only because our phonological system remains fluid until a couple of years after we have bonded with our mate," Anders explained. "That said, some of the languages I know will be impossible for me to speak now. The human vocal cords aren't able to create those sounds. You wouldn't enjoy hearing them anyway," he added with a grin.

"You mean like that sexy Eralgee screech?" I mumbled, remembering the nail on glass sound Anders had made when I'd startled him in that tentacle blob creature form.

He chuckled and gave me an amused sideways glance.

"But don't you get confused with so many languages in your head?" Wilson asked, tilting his head to the side. "I only speak three languages, and I often end up slipping a word from the wrong language into whatever sentence I'm saying."

That was actually a good question. With Anders speaking close to a hundred languages, it had to be a major clusterfuck in his mind.

"No, that is not a problem for us," Anders said, shaking his head. "However, the endless source of frustration is the limitation of one language compared to another. Some languages have a name for everything, down to the sound wrinkling paper makes versus the sound an aluminum sheet, or plastic does."

"They have words for that?" Naomi asked, surprised.

"They have words for the thickness, length, and density of one's eyelashes," Anders said with a smirk. "It gets annoying how insanely precise some of those languages are. That said, when you are ordering a specific part for an engine, receiving exactly what you wanted is really nice. However, when you're trying to tell a human doctor what the torture he's subjecting you to is doing, but there are not specific words to explain, you feel like killing someone," he ground through his teeth, making no mystery of how annoyed he had been.

"Dr. Spalding roughed you up?" Linda asked, her eyes lighting up with the curiosity of one about to hear some juicy gossip.

I chuckled and shook my head on his behalf.

"No, it wasn't here on Blyde Station," Anders explained. "We have to go through a thorough background check, psychological evaluation, and medical examination before we can go to our mate. They want to make sure we're not psychopaths and don't bring alien viruses that could decimate your population. Except, the doctor performing the test was a sadist who took advantage of your language's limitations to abuse me."

"Well," I said teasingly to my man, "it was about time that

humans be the ones probing the little grey men."

"Silver, my love, silver!" Anders corrected. "And I'm not little."

On this happy note, he dragged me to the dance floor. You guessed it; my sexy beast had learned a billion different dances. He did steal the show, but thankfully stopped short of doing head spins or any of those crazy acrobatic moves some dance groups performed.

Although I was having a blast, as a proper introvert, by the time we'd passed the three-hour mark at the party, I was starting to feel antsy and overwhelmed, needing to get back in my bubble. Anders naturally felt it and found a way to sneak us out of there, despite the 'elves' who did their best to herd us back inside.

On our way home, we passed a few couples, also sneaking away. A few of them had the revealing unstable gait of having downed one glass too many. Others had the wandering hands of those about to get naughty. One lone guy had the 'fuck my life, I have to be up early in the morning' look on his face. As for Anders and me, we definitely had the 'get down and dirty' mindset, even if our behavior revealed none of it—or so I hoped.

The door to my living unit no sooner closed behind us than Anders was already pushing me against the wall. It was a good thing we'd 'forgotten' to grab our gift bags on the way out. They'd probably be getting crushed under foot right now. Anders all but ripped the shirt off his back, discarding it somewhere in the general direction of the living room. With one hand, he pinned both of my wrists against the wall above my head while kissing me. His body, pressing against mine, kept me trapped.

There was something super sexy and exciting about feeling vulnerable and helpless while an insanely hot alien was having his way with you. And was he ever! His free hand was every-where at once, groping and fondling while his mouth plundered mine. However, as much as he was driving me wild with lust, I needed far more contact than this. Sensing my impatience and frustration, Anders released me long enough to rid me of my dress. But I pushed him back as soon as he tried to draw me back into his embrace.

"You had me sweating like a pig all evening on that dance floor," I protested, reluctantly batting away his gropey hands. "I need a shower before any kind of monkey business."

"A shower?!" Anders exclaimed, looking at me as if I'd just stolen his lunch money. "That's going to take forever! I will die waiting!"

I chuckled. "No, you drama queen. We can shower together," I said before biting his bottom lip.

"The shower is too small," he argued, leaning in to kiss me again.

I leaned my head back away from him and placed my fingers on his lips to keep him from kissing me. "Yours is small, but mine is bigger," I said, wiggling my eyebrows and deliberately emphasizing the innuendo.

He glared at me. Giggling, I smacked his behind, and then ran to my room while he gave chase. I never made it to the hallway leading to it before he swept me into his arms. He resumed kissing me while blindly making his way to my bedroom. Although he bumped into the walls a couple of times, even banging his pinky toe on the door frame, he still managed to reach our destination without me sustaining a single hit.

I almost felt guilty.

As soon as Anders put me back down, I kicked my shoes off and stripped out of my undies. How in the world he managed to remove his shoes, socks, belt, and pants, before I could even finish removing my earrings was beyond me. I ended up having to run away to try and get to my necklace. Once again, Anders caught me. This time, he unceremoniously tossed me over his shoulder like a sack of potatoes, then smacked my bum a good one.

Despite my head dangling behind his back, I managed to unclasp my necklace. As I extended my hand to place it on the dresser while Anders was walking past it, I caught a picture of us in the mirror. I burst out laughing at my pathetic self being carried to the shower, caveman-style, while my man's stiff cock was resolutely pointing at our destination.

He muttered something I didn't understand through my silly bouts of laughter. You'd think I was actually drunk when I'd only had a couple of glasses of wine with the meal. As soon as we entered the bathroom, Anders grunted his approval at the massive shower with his and hers shower heads. He put me down on my feet, just out of the way from the water before turning it on.

While waiting for the water to reach the appropriate temperature, my very horny alien pushed me against the cool tiles to resume kissing me again. I had never felt so wanted, so desirable… so beautiful even.

I barely felt him luring me under the water. We spent an eternity kissing and caressing each other under the raining water before Anders finally reached for the shower gel. If his touch had been incredibly soft before, with his flawless body and uncalloused hands, the soap made them even softer. It was like being caressed by silk. We soaped each other's front, our tasks rendered awkward by our inability to stop sucking each other's face. But me rubbing my soapy hand over his crotch appeared to bring Anders too close to his breaking point.

He spun me around with an angry growl and made me place my hands against the white tiles. "Move your hands from the wall, and I'll punish you," he whispered menacingly in my left ear.

My stomach flip-flopped, and my inner walls throbbed in response. He bit my nape, drawing a moan out of me while his hands circled around my front to fondle my breasts. As he began to rub his erect cock against the seam of my bum, I arched my lower back in to push out my bum and get more friction. His foot tapped the inner side of my right ankle, and I immediately complied, parting my legs wider. His left hand settled on my hip while the other abandoned my breast to slip down to my clit. I moaned again while he scissored it with two fingers before dipping them into my opening.

I was throbbing, aching to be filled. But Anders was determined to torture us for a while longer—something he seemed to enjoy a great deal. Unable to resist, I placed my hand over his to press it harder against my sex. His reaction was swift. Yanking his hand away, he slapped my right butt cheek with a loud, clapping sound. The blow resonated directly in my core, and I felt myself get even wetter while my inner walls contracted with impatience.

"Hands against the wall," Anders growled.

Although I complied, I seriously contemplated disobeying again, but this time deliberately. That sting had felt sinfully good. Reading my emotions, Anders chuckled. The fingers of his hand on my hip dug into my flesh, keeping it just below pain.

"You naughty, naughty girl," Anders whispered. "Looks like you will need to face some discipline in the future."

Yes, please?

I never got a chance to answer. I doubted my man expected one either. In an epic one-two punch, he smacked my bum again before impaling me with his cock. I couldn't even classify the weird squeal that came out of my mouth at the sudden fullness. It didn't matter. My alien lover went to town on me. Although we occasionally had gentle lovemaking, Anders had accurately guessed I like it rough, hard, and raw. And boy, did he deliver.

As he savagely rocked in and out of me, I met him thrust for thrust, leaning on the wall for support. Even as he had me slowly nearing the edge, my man peppered my ass with the occasional slap that sent bolts of fire exploding in the pit of my stomach.

My orgasm took me by surprise. It knocked my feet from under me and nearly sent me crashing face first into the shower wall.

But Anders had me covered.

He didn't just hold me up, he slipped his arms behind my knees and picked me up. My back pressed to his chest, my knees folded, he continued plowing in and out of me with a vengeance. Even as I rode the waves of ecstasy, his burning skin on my back, his labored breath in my ear, and his thick cock pummeling me had me cresting again.

I fell apart just as he shouted his own release. His shaft buried deep inside of me, his seed shot out into me, bathing my battered core while my inner walls squeezed every drop from him. Half-dazed with pleasure, and despite being folded up like a pretzel pinned on top of my man's hard rod, I reveled in the aftermath of intimacy. Anders always whispered words of love in my ears. His lips brushed over my nape, and his cheeks caressed my shoulder blade, making me feel cherished.

When he finally set me back on my feet and brought us under the water, I turned around and embraced him. I couldn't say how long we stayed like this in each other's arms while the lukewarm water rained on us. But at that moment, something settled in my heart. A part of me had known it from the first time we'd met, but now there was no more doubt in my mind.

I lifted my head to look at him. The intensity of his gaze, the vulnerability on his face, the mix of hope, love, and happiness that played on his features turned me upside down. He knew what I was going to say and was waiting with bated breath for the words to cross my lips, just like a woman whose boyfriend had suddenly kneeled before her, a tiny box in hand.

I cupped his face in my hands and gently caressed his cheeks while admiring the perfection of his features.

"I have dreamed of someone like you my whole life," I said in a voice shaking with emotion. "I'd given up hope. My crazy sister called for you. And you, my even crazier alien took a major leap of faith. You traveled to a whole new planetary system, to a weird species mostly foreign to you, just so that you could take a chance on me."

My throat incredibly tight, I swallowed painfully while my fingers slipped over the bony ridges of his crown before slipping through his hair.

"Unlike Lyrians, I can't feel your aura to tell me whether or not you're the one. But my heart knows," I continued in a whisper. "People will say this is too fast, too soon, that I don't really know you well enough. Maybe they're right, but I don't think so. I've never been so happy, so crazy about anyone than I am about you. You've not just made me fall head over heels in love with you, you've also taught me to love myself again. I love you, and I want you to bond with me, keep you forever, and be yours for as long as we both draw breath… if you will have me."

Seeing tears well in his eyes completely messed me up. I couldn't tell if his emotions, mine, or a mix of both were having that effect on him.

"I have loved you from day one," Anders said, his voice filled with emotion. "I would have bonded with you even if you had sent me away, because I could never belong to another. You are the other half of my soul. So yes, Kathleen, I want to bond with you. I want to keep you forever, and be yours until the end of our days."

"My beautiful Lyrian," I whispered and melted against him.

He kissed me, slowly, deeply, lavishing his love over me. I felt the moment he bonded, like a tingling at the back of my nape, and a soothing heat that seemed to wash over me from the top of my head down to the tip of my toes. Anders closed his eyes. A flash of light glowed through his eyelids, and a shiver coursed through him. I held my breath while he took in a deep one before slowly exhaling. He opened his eyes and smiled, looking at me with an air of wonder.

"We are one," he whispered.

EPILOGUE
KATHLEEN

In the weeks that followed, my bond with Anders further strengthened. At first, I'd feared bonding would change his personality. It was subtle, but he did change a bit. Although that term wasn't necessarily accurate. It was more that he became more affirmed in who he was.

For all his sweetness and eagerness to please me, Anders wasn't submissive; quite the opposite. I'd gotten a glimpse of his dominance, especially in the bedroom. As we grew closer and he got a better understanding of my likes and dislikes, openness and limits, he became bolder when testing them. And this didn't just apply to sex, but also to cooking, cheating when we played games, and plotting with Worf to drive me bonkers.

With my Kirdie experiment turning out to be a resounding success—which also earned me a big fat raise—I tried to sweet talk Anders into joining the xenobiology department. His empathic abilities would help us more easily interact with some of the alien creatures we worked with. However, Anders declined—but he offered to drop by whenever I felt his insight could help.

The Lyrian Matriarchy had a different role for him, which he embraced with delight. As the first of his kind in the Solar System, he would act almost as an Ambassador, establishing contacts with human mating agencies, identifying the human communities that struggled most with finding good, eligible partners, and spreading the word about the Empaths of Lyria. As he would have first-hand experience living among humans in our planetary system, he would be best suited to help design the appropriate marketing material to appeal to potential Seekers.

I hadn't realized how important that was until I'd seen some of their most successful marketing material used in Alpha Centauri. If they'd used that shit with humans, they'd be shamed out of the Solar System and labelled persona non grata for the next couple of centuries. Even when desperate, humans didn't like having that rubbed in their faces. In Alpha Centauri, Lyrians were considered as the best thing since warp travel had been achieved. They could get away with telling people to try their luck as a Seeker because, even though none of the other species wanted them, they could have the honor of being chosen by a Lyrian. Humans would kick you in the balls, and maybe even punch you in the throat with that kind of sales pitch.

The sympathy approach though promised to be a lot more effective. You've searched your whole life for Mr. Right, but they always fell short? Maybe you could find him among the Sons of Lyria. The majority of these Empaths, eager to please a single woman and fulfill her every desire, are dying alone for lack of compatible females on their home world. Find the man of your dreams today, and spare an Empath from a life of solitude.

Shameless.

And yet every spinster with a maze of cobwebs in her basement would sign up for it. I would have. Granted, I'd probably have started off with a fake username or something to test the waters before going all in. But who was I to deny these poor Empaths a chance at happiness… with me? That would have been unconscionable.

With Christmas now behind us and Valentine's Day fast approaching, Anders had plenty to keep him busy while I was off to work. He was all the more under pressure because, with his substantial wages paid by the Lyrian Matriarchy, Anders had booked us a two-week Valentine's honeymoon in Alpha Centauri, with a quick stop on Titan on our way back to say howdy to my sister and thank her for 'buying' him for me.

In the weeks leading up to our departure, a timid friendship developed between Anders and Wilson—his gym buddy. Although he never said as much, I suspected Anders was coaching him in letting his inner good guy come out, while burying the gloating asshole he'd been for so long. Naomi and he were still not officially an item. However, judging by the number of times she'd recently got 'conned' into going on a date with Wilson, it was only a matter of time.

Good on him!

Now, however, I'd have to find him a new nickname as The Dick no longer seemed appropriate.

But thoughts of Wilson would have to wait. As we embarked on the shuttle from the surface of Mars to the star cruiser that would take us to a whole new world I'd never dreamed of visiting one day, I addressed a silent thank you to my sister for changing the course of my boring life. My heart filled to bursting as I settled next to my mate, busy consoling Worf. My little Fudian was furious to have been forced to stay inside a travel cage until we reached the star cruiser, where he would regain his freedom—at least inside our suite.

Sensing my surge of emotions, Anders turned to look at me.

"I love you," I whispered.

"I love you, too, my wonderful little human."

THE END.

ANDERS

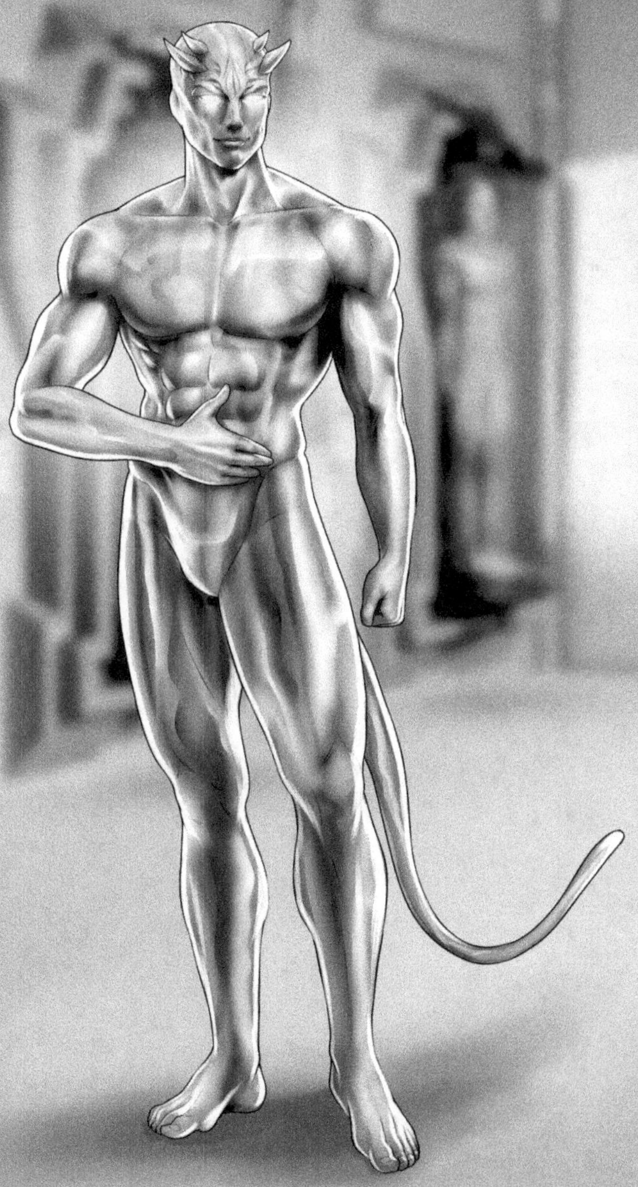

WORF

I Married A Naga
I Married A Birdman
I Married A Minotaur
I Married Wonjin
I Married A Merman
I Married A Dragon
I Married A Beast
I Married Krogal
I Married A Dryad
I Married An Incubus
I Married A Mothman

THE MIST
The Mistwalker
The Nightmare

DARK TALES
Bluebeard's Curse
The Hunchback

THE SHADOW REALMS
Destined to the Wraith
Destined to the Reaper

BLOOD MAIDENS OF KARTHIA
Claiming Thalia

VALOS OF SONHADRA
Unfrozen
Iced

EMPATHS OF LYRIA
An Alien For Christmas

OTHER
True As Steel
Alien Awakening
Heart of Stone

ABOUT REGINE

USA Today bestselling author Regine Abel is a fantasy, paranormal and sci-fi junkie. Anything with a bit of magic, a touch of the unusual, and a lot of romance will have her jumping for joy. She loves creating hot alien warriors and no-nonsense, kick-ass heroines that evolve in fantastic new worlds while embarking on action-packed adventures filled with mystery and the twists you never saw coming.

Before devoting herself as a full-time writer, Regine had surrendered to her other passions: music and video games! After a decade working as a Sound Engineer in movie dubbing and live concerts, Regine became a professional Game Designer and Creative Director, a career that has led her from her home in Canada to the US and various countries in Europe and Asia.

Facebook
https://www.facebook.com/regine.abel.author/

Website
https://regineabel.com

Regine's Rebels Reader Group

https://www.facebook.com/groups/ReginesRebels/

Newsletter

http://smarturl.it/RA_Newsletter

Goodreads

http://smarturl.it/RA_Goodreads

Bookbub

https://www.bookbub.com/profile/regine-abel

Amazon

http://smarturl.it/AuthorAMS